Jason

A Powerful New Beginning

BY

DEBBIE GONZALEZ

✻✻✻

HEMINGWAY
PUBLISHERS

*** *** ***

TABLE OF CONTENTS

❀❀❀

If you like Warlocks, Witches, Vampires, Werewolves, and Ghosts, this book is for you. This book is about a young 16-year-old boy who loves football and his family very much. He lives with Evelyn, his grandma, and Ava, his younger sister, who is 14, on a small family farm outside of Emory, Texas. Jason's mother passed away nine years ago, and Michael, his father, is always out of town for work, so selling the house and moving the kids in with his wife's mother was what Michael thought was best. Going to School and helping with his 14-year-old sister while working the family farm for grandma is a lot for a 16-year-old to handle. Helping with his sister, working on the farm, school, and sports all sounds like a stress-filled ordinary life, but things can always change in an instant, and for Jason, things are definitely about to change. Can he figure out the mystery behind this big change? Can he keep it a secret? What would happen if his family found out? Or do they know something he doesn't? That is what makes his life interesting, after all. See if you can guess what happens next, and this book will definitely have you guessing.

CHAPTER 1

Every morning starts the same for Jason. He wakes up at five in the morning, gets dressed, and then goes downstairs, where his grandma Evelyn is making breakfast, and he helps set the table. After eating breakfast, he's out the door to do his chores. He starts by feeding the three horses they have had for years and brushing them. He has always loved this part of the morning. You see, horses have always been Jason's favorite animal. His world always seems calm and centered when he is with them. It's easier to think about things because being around the horses makes him feel at peace. This is his happy place when everything else in his life seems out of place. His next chore is to let the chickens out and feed them so he can collect the eggs. Then, it's time to take out the trash. After completing the chores, he takes a shower and gets ready for school. He always tries to leave time for a long break before school, but some mornings, he just doesn't leave time for that. Being the only man around the house is hard. You have to do everything that a man is supposed to, no matter your age. It can be very stressful being raised on a farm, but he loves his farm very much. Taking care of the farm and his family gives him a purpose, and that is what keeps Jason going every morning.

As Jason walked through the door after doing chores this morning, things began to get busy very quickly. "Jason! Your sister can't find her dress shoes!" Evelyn yelled from the kitchen. He was used to helping his sister every morning. Evelyn was always busy making lunch for them to take to school, so he had to help out. "Can you just wear your tennis shoes, Ava?" Jason asked. "No, they won't go with my dress, and today is picture day!" Ava yelled. Ava and Jason were very popular among their friends. They were the face of the school and had many friends. Ava couldn't just wear anything because her picture would be the most popular one in the year book, and Jason's picture would lead the sports section because he was the star quarterback of Rains High School. Jason knew he had to hurry and find the shoes, or they would both be late.

"Keep looking downstairs, and I will check your room," Jason said. He looked everywhere: the closet, the hamper in the corner, behind the dresser, and even the bathroom, but there were no shoes. He finally thought to himself I bet they are under the bed; they have to be. I have checked everywhere else. Jason raised the bed skirt, and there he saw them nicely placed under the bed. "Found them!" Jason yelled. He gave the shoes to Ava, and she put them on, and they hurried to the car. Evelyn carried them to school every morning because they lived seven miles from town.

As Evelyn drove them to school, she wanted to ask Jason a huge question, but she knew what the answer would be. Today was Jason's 16th birthday. After careful thought, she decided to ask anyway. "What do you want for your birthday, Jason?" Evelyn asked very calmly. He hadn't really liked celebrating his birthday since his mom, Emma, passed away. He looked out the window but stayed very quiet for the whole ride. After pulling up at Ava's school, he got out and helped Ava out of the car like he does every morning. He helped her gather her things, gave her a hug, and told her he would be there waiting for her when she got out of school. They both watched as Ava walked inside, and then he got back in the car. As Evelyn started to drive away, he finally spoke to her. "I want to have a party; I miss my friends." Evelyn turned to look at him. "We can do that," Evelyn said. She didn't want to say it, but she was very excited.

"We can have the party on Saturday; that leaves three days to plan; does that sound good to you?" Evelyn asked. "Saturday is fine," Jason said as they pulled up at his school, which is just a few minutes walk across the yard from Ava's school. "Can we talk about it more after school, Grandma?" Jason asked. "Yes, I will come up with ideas while you're at school, and you do the same, and we will discuss all the ideas and come up with a full plan when you get home," Evelyn said. He smiled and got out of the car to head to school.

As he walked into the school, he ran into his best friend, Henry. They have been best friends since first grade. Jason tells Henry everything, and Henry tells Jason everything. They have always been more like brothers than friends. Their mothers were best friends growing up, which is how they met. Jason's mom and dad moved him away when he was just a little toddler, but after moving back, Jason met Henry for the second time, and they have been inseparable since then.

"We have a test today and I didn't study," Henry said.

"What test? Which class?" Jason asked.

"It's Mr. Malcom's science class," Henry said. Jason didn't have time to study himself; he was distraught because he was so close to failing that class already. Failing a test could get him kicked off the football team. "I have to know these answers, Henry; I can't fail this class," Jason said. *'I hope something happens, and he can't give us the tests,'* he thought to himself. Jason and Henry sit beside each other in the back of the room. Mr. Malcom began to hand out the tests, and Jason couldn't think of anything else but how the test questions had to be easy ones so he could pass. As the test started, he couldn't move. He was just too scared to look at the test. "Jason, this will be easy," Henry said. Jason looked over, and Henry was looking at the questions.

"They are things we learned years ago, Jason," Henry said. Jason thought to himself, oh, thank goodness, this must be one of those see what you know tests.

"OK, class, this isn't the test I wanted to hand out today, so we will be taking that one tomorrow. This is a review test that you should know all the answers to. If you don't, I guess you know what you should be doing between now and tomorrow before the real test." Mr. Malcom said.

Jason finished the test and took it to Mr. Malcom. Henry was right behind him. "That was the easiest test Mr. Malcom has ever given us, right Jason?" Henry asked.

"Yes," Jason said. Now, he was wondering why. It didn't make sense to him because that isn't the kind of test Mr. Malcom usually gives.

The day started to go by quickly as he started thinking about his party and how much fun it might actually be to celebrate it this year. Jason told Henry about the party, and they both spent the whole day planning everything. Jason also told Henry about his father being out of town and that he didn't think he would be able to come to the party. The boys then started inviting everyone, especially a girl named Sky. She has been Jason's crush since 3rd grade. They definitely had to invite her. On their way to lunch, they walked by the computer room and saw a man working on the copier. It was kind of odd that Jason got his wish, but the boys laughed it off as good luck. After walking into the lunch room and grabbing food, they went to their favorite seats. They always sit close to the door. You could see the whole lunchroom from their table because it was set on a platform that then had three steps that stepped down into the rest of the lunchroom. While the two were sitting and talking, Sky walked into the lunch room. Henry saw her and tapped Jason on the arm. He then pointed at Sky slightly so no one would notice. "Sky just walked in," Henry said.

"And?" Jason asked as he watched Sky going towards her table.

"Well, go talk to her; invite her to the party," Henry said.

"I can't just walk over and ask her to go to my party, can I? I mean, isn't it a little weird to do something like that at lunch?" Jason asked.

"Well, then, I will do it," Henry said as he stood up. "Henry, wait! No! Sit down! Ok, I'm going." Jason said as he stood up and grabbed Henry's shirt so he couldn't walk away. Henry sat back down. Jason slowly went down the stairs and walked over to Sky's table. "Umm, Sky," Jason said quietly. She looked up from her table, and her friends did as well. "Sky, I'm having a party this weekend at my place, and I would really like you to come; it's for my birthday," Jason asked.

"Like as your date?" Sky asked. His face turned a little pink.

"Yes, if you would like to?" Jason asked. She smiled as she could see how nervous he was, and she thought it was adorable.

"Yes, I will be your date, Jason," Sky said.

"Great! I mean, that's cool; I will see you at the party." Jason said as he slowly turned away. She laughed a little, but you could tell she liked Jason. His reaction to her answer made her smile even more. He walked back to his table, and as he sat down, Henry just looked at him. It was as if he thought Jason would faint or something. "Ok; what did she say?" Henry asked.

"She said yes; I can't believe she said yes," Jason said.

"Well, now I need a date, too," Henry said. "Who should I ask; maybe Sky's best friend?" Henry continued. "You could; best friends dating best friends; that could be interesting," Jason said. Henry got up and walked to the table where the girls were. "Hi Mya, I was thinking maybe we could go to the party together. Jason and I thought it would be kind of cool, you know, best friends dating best friends. What do you think?" Henry asked.

She looked at Sky as if she were waiting for her opinion. Sky just gave her a big smile and then looked back down at her food, which made Mya smile, too. "Yes, I will be your date, Henry," Mya said.

While the kids were at school, inviting people and making party plans, Evelyn had some planning to do on her own. To start, she needed to call Michael and tell him that his son had decided that he wanted a party this year. As she picked up the phone, she saw a text from Henry saying Jason really wanted his father to be at the party but didn't want to ask him. "I was just about to call him," Evelyn replied.

She dialed the number and waited for him to answer. On the 8th ring, he finally answered. "Hello, Evelyn," Michael said. "We need to talk… Jason wants a birthday party this year, and I'm giving him one here on the farm." Evelyn said. "What? He actually wants a party?" Michael asked.

"Yes, we are planning for this Saturday; can you make it?" Evelyn asked.

"I will do my best," Michael said. She wanted to tell him so much more than what she actually said, like, what do you mean you will try? You have been gone for months, and now your son wants a party for his birthday and wants you to come, and your answer is you will try? Instead, she just ended the call with, "Okay, well, we hope to see you here." She then looked at her locket with Jason's mom's picture inside and started talking to it; "Emma, my sweet daughter, if only you were here." She said softly to herself. "I'm not sure what to say anymore. Michael is gone, and eventually, Jason will start asking questions. What do I say to him?" After saying a few more things, she knew it was time to go. She wanted to say all this in person so badly, but knowing what was coming, she had to prepare.

It was now two in the afternoon, and the school day was almost over. During the free period, Jason decided to go sit by the tree in the backyard of the school because no one ever came back there. He was so ready to go home and take a nap. After getting up at five in the morning, who wouldn't be? He thought to himself, I just want to go home and lay down in my bed as he sat down under the big oak tree where he accidentally fell asleep. When he woke up, he was in his room. *'What?'* Jason thought. *How did I get home?* He went downstairs and saw Evelyn sitting there looking at her locket.

"Grandma, how did I get home, and where is Ava?" Jason asked. Evelyn didn't answer. Did she hear him? He walked in front of her and watched a tear go down her face. "I will take care of them, don't you worry?" Evelyn said. He looked around the room but didn't see anyone.

"Grandma, what are you crying for, and who are you talking to?" She still said nothing. Evelyn looked up at the clock right behind him as if she were looking through him and said, "It's almost time to pick up the kids."

He then heard another voice say, "Please contact me later and tell me how he handles it." At that time, he turned around to see who was there but saw no one. Then, he saw the time on the clock. It was 2:45. That's when he was supposed to head over to Ava's school and wait for her to get out. What was going on? He started to panic. He was at school and woke up at home. Grandma couldn't see or hear him, and he needed to be there for his sister. He felt as if it were a horrible dream. He finally convinced himself he was dreaming and needed just to wake up. He then woke up under the tree. He looked around and said, "Oh, thank God it was just a dream, well more like a nightmare." He then checked the time, and it was 2:55. He jumped up and ran to his sister's school, making it there with two minutes to spare. He started thinking about his dream and how crazy it was. *'Was that a dream,'* he thought, *'Could I have really been home?'* Then he laughed and thought it was not possible. How could I have been home? He was drained from the run, so he sat down to wait for his sister and continued to think about his dream.

Ava walked out and saw Jason and ran to him like every day to hug him. He gave her a hug as Evelyn pulled up. Jason and Ava walked to the car, and he helped her get in the back seat. When he finally got in the front, he saw Evelyn crying, which made him think his dream was even more real. Should he ask? "No, he thought to himself. She will think I'm crazy and send me to a shrink, and if my dream was somehow real, I would end up in a lab somewhere." He was quiet the whole way home. He didn't really know what to say because all he could think about was that dream. After they got home, he went straight to his room, sat down on his bed, and started taking his shoes off. He then started thinking of that morning. His sister's shoes were under her bed, just like he pictured them. Then the test he hoped something would happen so that Mr. Malcom couldn't give them the test. Then he fell asleep thinking of being home and then woke up at home, but it was like he was a ghost.

"Could all of this be a coincidence? Or was I making it happen?" Jason thought. He lay down looking at the ceiling, thinking about the whole day and how everything went his way. "I must be going crazy. It's impossible to think I did all of this." Jason said. He grabbed his phone and called Henry.

"Henry, you need to come to my house right now; we need to talk," Jason said.

"Are you ok, man? You know what, never mind, I'm on my way." Henry said.

He then went outside to wait on Henry. He sat down on the porch steps and tried to figure everything out.

As Henry pulled up on his dirt bike, he saw Jason sitting outside on the steps. "Jason?" Henry said. Jason looked at him for a second, very confused.

"Something happened today; I'm not sure what exactly, but when I was at school, I fell asleep and had a weird dream. I was at home, and I saw my Grandma sitting and looking at my mom's picture in her locket. She was crying, and she could not hear me or see me, but then I woke back up at the school, and things just hadn't seemed right since. I think I'm going crazy, Henry. The things that have happened today have all seemed normal until that dream. Then the other things that happened today weren't so normal anymore." Jason said.

Henry looked at Jason. "Everyone has crazy dreams, its normal," Henry said.

"Not like this," Jason said and then paused for a long time, and then he finally spoke. "It felt so real. What if I somehow came home in my sleep?" Jason asked.

"You mean like an out-of-body experience?" Henry asked as he laughed.

"I'm serious, Henry; something happened! Explain my grandma crying when she picked Ava and me up earlier from school if you think I'm going crazy," Jason said in a firm voice.

"OK, OK, calm down; let's talk about it tomorrow. I will do some research tonight and see what I can figure out. I have to get home before my mom starts to wonder where I am." Henry said. As

Henry left, Jason started thinking about what would happen if he went to sleep.

'Will I end up somewhere else?' Jason thought as he walked upstairs.

He decided that he wasn't going to sleep. *I'm going to make myself stay up all night and try to figure things out. If I'm crazy, I will tell grandma. If I'm not, well, I guess I will figure that out later.'* Jason thought to himself. He then went to the kitchen and gathered up drinks, food, and many other things for a long night, which he had to hide out of sight for when his grandma came in. He wasn't sure he wanted her to ask questions just yet. As he sat down on his bed, his phone began to ring; it was Henry. "Hey, how did the research go so far?" Jason asked.

"I'm not sure; I started researching your dream first, and it's kind of creepy because there are actually others that say they have had things similar happen to them," Henry said.

"Like what?" Jason asked.

"Well, some say it's called astral projection, while others say it's all in your head," Henry replied.

"That's not creepy. How does that creep you out?" Jason asked.

"That's not the creepy part; some of these people are dead now," Henry answered.

"How did they die?" Jason asked.

"Well, it depends on which one you want to know about. Car crashes, house burning down in the middle of the night, just a whole bunch of random accidents." Henry said.

Suddenly, Jason had an idea. "I got to go; call me with any new information," Jason said. He ran to the kitchen, grabbed a bowl, and ran back to his room. He sat down at his desk and flipped the bowl over with the bottom up. Then he started thinking. '*If I made the shoes appear this morning, I could make something else appear under this bowl right now.*' Jason thought. He then shut his eyes and thought, '*when I lift the bowl, there will be an apple under it.*' He then slowly lifted the bowl and opened his eyes. "No apple; maybe I was making a big deal of nothing," Jason said to himself. He then decided to try again, so he set the bowl back down and thought it again. '*When I lift the bowl, there will be an apple.*' Just about that time, he heard his grandma coming, which scared him, and as he grabbed the bowl to hide it, he knocked it off onto the floor, and an apple fell off the desk as well.

Just then, he knew everything that had happened that day couldn't have been a coincidence, and he now knew what he could do and that it wasn't in his head, but Evelyn was still walking up the stairs. So he shoved everything under the desk, grabbed his laptop, and pulled up school work right as she walked in. "We didn't have much time to talk today; how was your day? Did anything interesting happen today?" Evelyn asked.

He wanted to tell her everything, but he was scared she would think he was crazy. "No, it was a very boring day," Jason said.

"You can tell me anything; you do know that, right?" Evelyn asked.

"I know, Grandma," Jason answered. "Come down stairs so we can talk about the party," Evelyn said.

"Can we talk about it tomorrow, Grandma? I'm really tired." Jason said.

"That's fine. You get some rest. OK," Evelyn said. As she left the room, Jason grabbed his phone and called Henry. "I did it, Henry; I made it happen," Jason said.

"Made what happen?" Henry asked.

"Come over; my grandma is going to sleep soon; be quiet and come straight upstairs," Jason said.

He was still at his desk when Henry walked in. He held his hand up, holding the apple. "I made this apple appear," Jason said. "I have been trying to figure this out since you left, and at first, I thought I was going crazy, but now I know for sure I'm not," Jason said.

"Ok, so it's eleven at night, and I rode my bike over here to see a magic trick," Henry said.

"It's not a trick, Henry. I really did it; watch." Jason said. He tried to make a new apple appear, but it didn't work this time. "Why isn't it working?" Jason said.

"Maybe because you're crazy," Henry said while he laughed. "You just need to get some sleep," Henry said.

Jason started getting upset. He then tried again, "There will be an apple when I lift this bowl!" Except this time, he said it out loud and with powerful feelings. When he lifted the bowl, they saw four apples. Henry walked over to the desk slowly. "How did you do that?" Henry asked as he picked up an apple.

"I think I'm starting to figure it out," Jason said. "I think it's tied to my emotions, like when I'm scared or upset; just not sure what it is," Jason said. They started going over everything that happened that day, beginning with that morning with Ava's shoes. When he found the shoes he was very stressed out because he thought they were going to be late for school. Then the test, he didn't want to fail the test; he needed to pass, so again, he was stressed, but what about when he was sleeping? That is the only part of the day that they can't seem to figure out. "Let's practice with it," Henry said. The boys then stayed up most of the night trying to figure out all of his triggers and having him bring different things into the room from the kitchen with his new found gift. Henry then had an idea.

"Let's see how strong your power is; bring my laptop over from my house," Henry said.

Jason thought about it for a second and decided it was worth a try. So he began picturing Henry's laptop sitting before him on his desk when suddenly it appeared there on the desk. Henry was very still and couldn't stop looking at his laptop. It was almost as if he was in shock. "Are you ok, Henry?" Jason asked.

Henry jumped up from his seat and scared Jason. "Do you know what this means!" Henry yelled.

"What! And keep your voice down before you wake everyone." Jason said. "You're like a warlock or something," Henry said.

"Really, a warlock. Those are not real." Jason said as he turned away from Henry. Even though he was thinking Henry might be right.

"Ok, then, how did you do that? You're the one that just brought my laptop from my desk to yours, which is a mile down the road, and you don't think you might be a warlock or even a wizard or something?" Henry asked.

"We should go to sleep; it's three in the morning," Jason said. He didn't want to answer Henry. He already felt like a freak. If he admits it, then he knows that it will definitely make him one. So the boys went to sleep thinking about Jason's new found powers. If they only knew that was just the beginning.

CHAPTER 2

Jason and Henry woke up the next morning to the sound of the phone ringing in the kitchen. They could hear Evelyn as she answered the phone. "Hello," Evelyn said.

"I bet it's my mom. I never went back home last night, and I didn't call or leave a note. She is probably very mad at me for leaving last night." Henry said. At that moment, the boys heard her coming upstairs. As the door swung open, the boys prepared to be in trouble.

"Oh, thank God! Young man, your mom just called, and she was very worried. She didn't know where you were. I told her I would check to see if you were here. Why didn't you tell your mom you were coming over here?" Evelyn asked.

He couldn't answer with the truth, saying Jason had powers and he just had to see them, so he had to think of something quick. "I was helping Jason plan for his party; I planned to go back home, but I fell asleep," Henry replied.

"Well, you need to go home, get ready for school, and call your mom on the way out," Evelyn said. As Henry left, Jason was still thinking about everything that had happened that night. He realized that he had slept for a good while and had never had a dream. At least he didn't remember if he did. He then looked over and saw that Henry left his laptop and thought maybe instead of bringing things to me, I could send them back. He closed his eyes and started picturing the laptop sitting back on Henry's desk at his house. When he opened his eyes, the laptop was gone. He was finally getting the hang of his powers and began to wonder what else he could do. More importantly, where did the powers come from. He jumped as his phone rang; it was Henry. "Hey, did you make it home?" Jason asked.

"Yes, and my laptop is back; how did you send it back?" Henry asked.

"Same way I brought it to my house; I think I'm getting the hang of these powers. I will see you at school." Jason said. He got dressed as he did every morning to go downstairs to eat with Evelyn and Ava. As he got downstairs, Evelyn looked worried. "What's wrong, grandma?"

Jason said. "My ring fell down the drain," Evelyn said. This wasn't just any ring. It was her wedding ring from Jason's grandpa. They were married for a long time. He knew what the ring looked like, so he knew he could get it back. He went to his room and pictured the ring in his hand. Before he knew it, the ring was sitting there in his palm, but now he had a problem. How would he explain this to Evelyn? Should he just tell her the truth or come up with a plan?

Jason hid the ring for now and hurried back to eat so he could get to his chores. As he got ready for school and went downstairs, his sister was not in her uniform, which she should be, and was looking pretty, and his grandma smiled at him.

"What is going on? Is there something I don't know?" Jason asked.

"You're not going to school today," Evelyn said. "What; why; is something wrong?" Jason asked.

"We are going party shopping and then having a birthday dinner with just us," Evelyn said. Jason was pleased about party shopping. It would be his first party in 9 years. Jason finished eating and went out to do his chores. He was very happy today and started using his powers for everything he could think of. He needed to practice. He used his powers to find the horse brush in the barn; he even used his powers to collect the eggs from the hen house. His chores went by a lot faster today, and he had so much fun. When he got to the house, he saw a car parked in the yard. A car he had never seen before.

As he walked inside, he heard a man talking in the kitchen. He slowly walked around the corner to peek and saw his father with Ava at the table. "Well, hello, son; I was told you wanted a party this weekend," Michael said.

"Yes, sir," Jason said. "What are you doing here, though; don't you have to work?" Jason asked.

"Not today; I told them I needed to go see my son because he was going to be a man soon, and I have missed too much of his life already," Michael continued. "I saw you in the barn, and you looked quite busy, so I decided to come in the house and give you some time to finish your chores,"

Jason looked at his father for a second and then went upstairs to shower. He thought about what his dad said all the way upstairs. His dad came to the barn. Did he see Jason use his powers? If he did, why would he be so calm about it? He couldn't ask these questions without answering his father's questions, and he knew what one of those questions would be. Why was he asking so many questions?

"Why don't you go get your things ready, Ava? I need to talk to your father." Evelyn said.

"Ok, Grandma," Ava said. As she left the room, Evelyn got up and grabbed a couple of cups from the cabinet to make tea.

"You know he is sixteen now," Evelyn said.

"I know; how is he doing?" Michael asked.

"Well, he hasn't said much, but I think something has happened. He seemed different when I picked him up from school yesterday, and then last night, his best friend Henry snuck over and stayed the night. I'm sure they were talking most of the night." Evelyn said.

"Should I talk with him about it?" Michael asked.

"Talk with him, yes, but not with specifics. Just see if maybe he will mention it to you first." Evelyn answered. Jason was already out of the shower and coming down the stairs. He heard everything they said and went back to his room as he heard his father coming. Just as he sat down at his desk, he heard a knock on the door.

"Jason, can I come in?" Michael asked.

"Yes," Jason said. All Jason could think about was what his father knew and what he should say. What were these "specifics" Evelyn was talking about? "Hi, Dad; I'm glad you came," Jason said.

"Me too; how is school going? You're still in football, right?" Michael asked as he sat down on Jason's bed. "It's good, and yes, I'm still in football. I plan to play till I graduate if nothing happens." Jason replied.

"What would happen?" Michael asked. Jason wanted to say well, I have powers now, and I might send the ball to China if I'm not careful, but he didn't say anything at all.

"You know you can talk to me about anything, right?" Michael reassured. "Yes, Dad, I know," Jason said. Jason started thinking again. Could he tell his dad, though? His dad would probably flip out and think he was crazy.

"Your mom had a secret too, and she was scared to tell me, but when she finally did, she felt better because I actually took the news well," Michael said.

"What was the secret?" Jason questioned.

"She told me to wait till you're ready before I tell you, and I'm not sure you are," Michael said.

Jason thought for a minute about what to say. "What made you okay with Mom's secret?" Jason asked.

"Because I had one of my own, and when I think you are ready, I will tell you them both," Michael said. "Now finish getting ready and come to the kitchen so we can get this day started," Michael said while smiling. Michael started walking out of the bedroom when Jason stopped him.

"Dad, when you came to the barn, why didn't you come in?" Jason asked.

"Well, you seemed busy brushing the horses, so I didn't want to get in the way. Besides, it looked like you had everything under control." Michael said.

"When did you show up at the barn? What was I doing as you first looked in?" Jason asked.

"You were tying up the horses, getting ready to brush them; why?" Michael asked.

"No reason, I was just wondering," Jason said. Michael smiled and walked out the door. "Come down when you're ready," Michael said.

"Ok, and Dad, I do have a secret too, but I'm not sure I'm ready to share it," Jason said.

"That's ok. I will be here when you're ready to talk about it." Michael said as he shut the door. Jason sat there for a minute, thinking about what his dad had said about his mom and dad having a secret and why he couldn't tell him yet. He knew he would have to figure it out because it just might be the answer to what was happening to him. Michael walked into the kitchen and looked at Evelyn.

"Well," Evelyn said.

"You are right. Something has happened, but he won't tell me what." Michael said.

"Just give him time; he will open up. He has questions already, I'm sure." Evelyn said.

As Jason walked into the kitchen, everyone was getting ready to leave. "Alright, everyone, going party shopping. Get in the car!" Evelyn yelled. Jason and Ava raced to the car. They were already having fun, and the day just started.

"Where are we going first?" Ava asked.

"To the mall; they should have almost everything we need," Evelyn said. Evelyn started driving, and everyone sang to the music on the radio. Jason was actually having a perfect day, even with everything on his mind. As they pulled into the mall, he wondered what else he could do with his powers and stared off into space. "Jason, you ok?" Michael asked.

"Yes," Jason answered.

"Well I said your name like four times before you noticed. Are you sure you don't want to talk about whatever is bothering you?" Michael asked.

"Not yet, but when I do, I will let you know," Jason said as he got out of the car. As they walked into the mall, they saw so many stores.

"I'm going to go into this jewelry store and get my ring cleaned; I dropped it down the sink earlier," Evelyn said. Jason turned to look at the ring in her hand. That was the ring he had just used his powers to get out of the drain and hide in his room. How did his grandma have it? Did she find it in his room? Why didn't she ask him how he found it?

"Is that the only one you dropped down the drain?" Jason asked.

"Yes, but I was able to get it out," Evelyn said. He knew that was a lie because he had the ring. Well, he did have it. Jason now knew something was happening, but no one wanted to tell the truth, especially him.

"How did you get it out?" Jason asked. She didn't answer and stayed quiet.

"Look, I want to go play games!" Ava yelled. Jason looked up and saw the arcade. "Yeah, that sounds fun. Can I take her to play while you two shop for a bit?" Jason asked.

"Sure. You two have fun." Evelyn said. Ava grabbed his hand, and they ran to the arcade. She started playing games, and Jason sat down to text Henry. "My dad told me that he and my mom both have a secret that I'm not ready to know about yet. What do you think that means?" Jason texted. He looked up and saw Ava still playing. Then his phone beeped so he looked back down and it was Henry.

"I'm not sure, but what if it's the same secret you have?" The screen showed this message. He then told Henry everything that happened that morning. Then he looked up and saw some guys standing around Ava. One guy who looked way older than her was trying to get her number. He got mad and walked over to them. "Are you hitting on my fourteen-year-old sister?" Jason asked.

"Well, hi there, my name is Mike."

"I didn't ask for your name. I asked if you were trying to get my sister's number?" Jason said. They all looked at Jason. "I think you should walk away." Jason then took Ava's arm and pulled her over behind him. One of the guys then decided to swing at him, and he ducked and then pushed the guy, who flew back into the arcade machine behind him. After he got up, all the guys ran away.

"How did you push him so far, Jason?" Ava asked.

"Eat your vegetables, Ava. That's how." Jason said with a confused look. Honestly, he had no idea how he did that. "Let's go find Grandma and Dad." They walked around the mall for what seemed like an hour, looking for them.

"I'm hungry," Ava said. "Alright, let's go to the food court, and I will find you something to eat," Jason said. As they sat down at the food court, he saw Evelyn and Michael. They were sitting at the coffee shop. Ava grabbed her food and began to eat. Jason just watched them and wondered what they were talking about. About 30 minutes later, Evelyn texted them both to meet her and their father at the car when they were ready. Evelyn and Michael then stood up and walked toward the exit. Ava finished eating, and they both headed to the car. When they got there, Evelyn held up a huge bag. "I got you a present, Jason," Evelyn said.

"Thanks, grandma," Jason said.

"Where would you like to go eat, Jason?" Michael asked.

"I would honestly just like to pick up some pizza and go home so Henry can come over and join us if that's ok?" Jason asked.

"That sounds like a great idea," Michael said. They then drove their long trip back home. Jason texted Henry and told him they were heading home and that he was invited for pizza.

As they pulled up at home, Henry was already there on the porch waiting. "Hello, everyone," Henry said as he stood up and ran to the car. "How was your trip?" Henry asked while kind of laughing. Henry has always been the clown type.

"It was a long one. Can you and Henry help us get everything out of the trunk, Jason?" Michael asked.

"Yeah," Jason replied, even though he hadn't seen them with bags earlier at the coffee shop. Evelyn opened the trunk and it was full of stuff. There must have been 30 bags crammed in there. '*I guess they brought all this out to the car before they got coffee,*' Jason thought. They started carrying bags into the house, and when they got inside Evelyn asked them to unpack the bags and set everything on the couch. While unpacking the bags, Jason started seeing things that he didn't think he could get at the mall.

"Henry, have you ever seen this streamer at the mall before?" Jason asked.

"No, but surely they have it somewhere, I guess, or they wouldn't have found it," Henry answered.

"Hurry up, we need to go talk," Jason whispered worriedly. The boys finished unpacking and ran upstairs. He then took out his phone and showed Henry the picture he had taken of the streamer. "Why did you do that?" Henry asked.

"Because tomorrow I'm skipping school to go look for this streamer," Jason said.

"Let me guess, you want me to go too?" Henry asked.

"I'm serious, Henry. Something is going on with my family, and I'm going to figure it out. They are hiding something from me, and I want to know what it is." Jason said.

"Boys, come back down here for pizza!" Evelyn yelled. Henry started to run out the door when Jason grabbed him.

"Don't tell them what we know," Jason said.

"And what exactly would that be, Jason?" Henry asked with a sarcastic look. Henry then turned around and walked out the door, and went downstairs. Jason stood there for a minute and then decided to go eat as well. As he was walking downstairs, he got a weird feeling that someone was watching him. He slowly continued into the kitchen but then heard a noise outside. He turned and opened the front door and didn't see anyone. At this point, he really felt like he was going insane. "You better get in here, man, before I eat all the pizza!" Henry yelled while laughing. Jason turned toward the kitchen but couldn't shake the feeling of being watched. He decided to join the others and see what he could find out.

As they all sat down to eat, he felt happy. He was watching everyone sitting around the table, eating and laughing. He thought to himself, this is my family, secrets or not; this is where I want to be. "What are we doing after dinner, Grandma?" Jason asked.

"Well, I figured we would start getting the barn ready," Evelyn said.

"That's where we have decided to let you have the party. You will have the barn to yourselves without us standing over you but close enough to keep an eye on all of you," Michael said.

"This party is going to be awesome," Henry said.

Jason looked at him and smiled. "I couldn't agree more," Jason said. He had a plan for when they finished eating. He wanted him and Henry to head to the barn before everyone else. As soon as they finished eating, he looked up at Evelyn and asked if he and Henry could get a head start on decorating while Evelyn and Michael cleaned up.

"Sounds like a plan to me. Try to put most of the lights in the loft." Evelyn said. They grabbed everything and continued to the loft.

"I'm going to try something," Jason continued. "Earlier at the arcade, when I shoved this guy for flirting with Ava, I think I sent him flying with my powers as well."

"Wait! What!! Who was flirting with Ava?" Henry asked. Jason could see he was full of anger.

"Are you ok, and why are you being weird?" Jason asked.

"Nothing; I just don't like that someone was messing with Ava," Henry said. He stood there looking at Henry for a minute with a confused, aggravated look. "You're into my sister, aren't you?" Jason asked.

"What? No... Look are we doing these decorations or what?" Henry confusedly asked.

"Yes, my plan is to use my powers to hang the lights if I can. If I really did push that guy with my powers, then I should be able to move the lights," Jason replied and then had Henry hold the lights across his arms, attempting to move them with his mind.

"It's not working. Maybe you need to replicate the feelings you had earlier when you threw that guy." Henry interrupted.

"You mean anger, but how do I get mad on command?" Jason asked.

"Think about what the guy said or did," Henry said. Jason stood there for a long time trying to get angry, and he just couldn't pull the feelings up. It was starting to feel hopeless, and the boys were about to give up until Henry said something stupid. "I lied. I do like your sister. I honestly wish I would have thought about asking her to be my date first before asking Mya." Henry said. Suddenly, Jason looked at him, and Henry flew over the rails of the loft and fell below into the hay.

"Oh my God, Henry, are you ok?" Jason shouted as he ran downstairs to check on Henry. He was slowly crawling out of the hay.

"Yeah, I'm alright," Henry said in a very shaky voice. He then pushed Henry again except without his power this time. He didn't want to hurt Henry.

"Why didn't you tell me the truth, Henry?" Jason asked.

"Calm down, man. I was just trying to make you mad." Henry said. He looked at Henry and then looked away. He couldn't help but think of what Henry said. He had a feeling Henry might actually have feelings for Ava; they were not that far apart in age, after all. Ava's birthday was just four days after his party, and he thought she might ask Henry to be her date if she liked him as well, but he had to let it go for now. He felt responsible for Ava since their mom passed, and thinking of her dating bugged him. He decided to keep an eye on them. "Well, at least we know how you pushed him so far," Henry said.

"Who was pushed?" Michael asked from just behind the door.

"Dad, I didn't see you there," Jason answered.

"Where are the decorations?" Michael asked.

"Oh, they are in the loft," Henry replied. They all went upstairs to start decorating, but the boys never answered Michael's question about who got pushed. They knew there would be too many questions tied to that one answer. It's best to take his mind off of what he asked. Soon, Evelyn walked in to help decorate and they all had a really great time decorating. Before they knew it, the place looked great, and only one more day till the party.

Now, they could focus on what to wear and wonder about their dates. Jason was very worried because he asked Sky before he knew he had these crazy powers that he was still learning to control. What if something went wrong that night, and he hurt her? So many things were going through his mind. "I'm going to go grab a drink. Does anyone want anything?" Henry asked.

"Sure, bring the pizza, too," Michael said.

As he walked into the house, Ava was standing there with a tray. She was already headed outside with drinks. He bumped right into her, and she dropped the tray. "I'm so sorry, Ava. I didn't see you. I will help you clean this up; let me get a towel." Henry said. He ran to grab the towel and came back and Ava was picking up the pieces when he heard her say ouch.

"What happened?" Henry asked.

"I just cut my finger, but I'm fine," Ava said. "Let me see," Henry said.

"No, I'm fine," Ava said.

He grabbed her arm. "Stop being stubborn, Ava," Henry said as he pulled her to him. She fell against him a little. As she looked at him, he knew for sure that Jason was right. He had feelings for Ava, and when Jason found out, he would hurt him. He quickly looked at her finger and then turned her loose. "You were right; you're fine," Henry said. Then he turned around and went to get the pizza. "Let's grab the drinks, and then we will clean this up later," Henry said. He walked over to the table, grabbed the pizza, and turned back around. She was still looking at him as if she had feelings, too, but she was also young and scared to say it. They grabbed the drinks and pizza, then went to the barn. They talked and ate pizza under the lights as a normal family, but as you know by now, they are far from normal. As it got late, Evelyn sent Henry home and Jason and Ava to bed.

Ava couldn't stop thinking about Henry, and she was also confused because she felt the same thing she knew he felt as he took her hand earlier that day. She snuck into Jason's room after he was asleep and copied Henry's number into her phone. She then went to her room and texted Henry. "Why did you look at me like that, Henry?"

"Ava?" Henry asked.

"Yes, it's Ava. I don't understand what happened earlier." Ava texted back.

"I was just worried about you, Ava," Henry answered.

"That was not a worried look, Henry. You should just tell me the truth. I know you felt something, too, but you're just scared to admit it. When you decide you're done being scared, let me know." Ava said. The two left it at that, but Ava made up her mind that if Henry had feelings for her, she would make him admit them to her. She had her own planning to do before the party.

Jason was sleeping peacefully until he started having a dream about his mother. It started with his mother sitting on the side of his bed and telling him to wake up. He opened his eyes to see his mother, and it frightened him. He wasn't sure if he was dreaming or not. It felt so real. "I need to tell you something, Jason. I have been watching you, and I know your secret. It's ok to be scared, son but you need to know you're in danger. I know you don't understand right now, but you need to tell your grandmother and your dad about your powers. You will be surprised how understanding they can be. It's important to learn your strength soon because you are being watched. I know you're scared, son, but you need to stay focused and watch your surroundings. I love you, and I know I will see you soon. This will all make sense later, but for now, just be careful." Emma said. All he could do was sit there and look at her and try to wake up. He felt as if this was a nightmare, and he didn't understand. Ava heard a noise from Jason's room so she ran in to check on him and found him moving around as if he was having a bad dream. She ran to his side and started shaking him. "Jason, wake up! Please wake up! It's just a dream!" Ava yelled.

At that moment, Jason's mom started to reach for him in his dream, which made him jump from fear. He woke up fast, set up in bed, threw his hand out, and yelled No. While doing so, he threw

Ava against the wall with his powers. "Ava?" Jason asked as he looked really hard to see who it was. "I'm so sorry. Did I hurt you?" He asked as he jumped up from bed and ran to Ava.

"How did you do that, Jason?" Ava asked.

"Never mind that Ava; are you ok?" Jason asked again as he helped her to her feet.

"I think so. Now answer me. How did you do that?" Ava asked again. He sat down on the bed and put his head in his hands with a sigh because he knew he had to tell her. He then set her down and told her everything.

"Are you going to say something, Ava?" Jason asked.

"What do you want me to say? This is a lot to take in, Jason. I mean, you have powers. What am I supposed to think?" Ava asked.

"Just keep it between us, please. Ava, you're my sister and it has been killing me that I felt I couldn't tell you. I honestly think it is better that you know now." Jason said. She just sat there for a minute thinking.

"I will keep your secret because you are my brother. Who knows, this might turn out to be kind of fun." She said with a smile as she got up and walked to the door. He just smiled back. They told each other goodnight and went to bed with a lot on their mind.

CHAPTER 3

Here is the day before the party. Jason had no intentions of going to school today and neither did Ava. Jason was sitting on his bed thinking when Ava knocked and walked in. They wanted to figure out what was going on with him. They were still in his room when Evelyn woke up. She heard them talking and decided to look in to see if everything was ok. "Hello, you two, and good morning. How about some breakfast before school?" Evelyn asked, even though she fixed breakfast every morning.

"Yes, Grandma, we are starving," Ava said. Jason knew they had to tell Henry. He picked up his phone and began to call Henry.

Well, Henry was having a crazy morning as well. "Mom, where are Dad's old suits?" Henry asked.

"They are in the attic," Sandy said. Henry headed to the attic and ended up there for an hour, going through many boxes. He found some exciting things that proved Jason wasn't the only unordinary person in his family. He knew he had to call Jason. At that time, Henry's phone rang. It was Jason. He called to tell Henry about his dream, and after Jason rambled for about five minutes, Henry finally interrupted. "Listen, Jason, I'm sorry to interrupt, but forget about the streamer. You need to come to my house. I have got to show you something."

"I was going to skip school anyway because I have to figure this out before tomorrow; let's meet at the school. Actually, let's meet at Ava's school. I will tell Grandma I want to walk from there." Jason said.

"How are we going to get from the school to my house?" Henry asked.

"Don't worry, I have an idea," Jason said.

"Oh great, we know how the last idea turned out," Henry said.

"Just meet me there, Henry!" Jason said in a frustrated voice. Evelyn yelled breakfast was ready, so Ava told Jason she would see him down there and went downstairs. He sat there thinking about his idea. He was going to attempt to send all three of them to Henry's house. He started wondering if he could even do it. If his dream was real he had a great power that could do almost anything. '*Let's start small*,' he thought to himself. He closed his eyes and pictured himself in his bathroom and soon felt a strange feeling, almost like his whole body went numb, and when he opened his eyes he was in the bathroom. He looked at himself in the mirror and exclaimed, "I can do this." He then went downstairs to join Ava for breakfast.

"Morning, son; I'm going to give you a ride to school so we can talk," Michael said.

"What about Ava?" Jason asked.

"Evelyn is still taking her," Michael said. Ava looked at Jason with a worried look because she really wanted to go with him to Henry's. She was curious about what was going on with Jason. At that moment, he looked at her and smiled, so she knew he would find a way to take her with him. He sat down to eat and texted Henry about the change of plans. They would meet at the high school and then go to Ava's school. After breakfast, Jason did his chores then it was time to grab their things and head out the door for school. Ava was looking for her backpack so she asked for Jason's help as always. They went upstairs to check her room, and Jason just had to show her one of his powers. They were standing in her room, and he told her to hold her hands out, and he placed his hands under hers, and then he told her to shut her eyes. He then made the backpack appear in their hands. "Open your eyes, Ava," Jason said.

"That is so awesome. What else can you do? How does it work, though?" Ava asked.

"I'm not sure yet, but I hope we get a few answers today," Jason said. They went back down to the kitchen and saw Evelyn talking to Michael. They didn't hear what they said, but they knew they were whispering for a reason. Evelyn then took Ava to the car, and they left for the school. Michael then asked Jason if he was ready. As they were walking to the car Jason decided to try and get some information. "Dad, can I ask you a question?"

"Sure, son," Michael replied.

"Do you have dreams about mom?" Jason asked.

"Yes, I do, and some of them feel very real. Why? Are you having dreams about her?" Michael asked.

"Only one, and it was last night, and it felt real and was a little scary. It's probably because I miss her, right?" Jason asked.

"We all miss her. Maybe it would help to talk about the dream and tell me what happened." Michael said as they got in the car.

"There really isn't much to talk about. It didn't really make sense. She was telling me I was in danger and that I was being watched, which was the creepy part." Jason said as they pulled out of the driveway. Michael pulled over on the side of the road and looked at him.

"Being watched? What do you mean? Did she say who?" Michael asked.

"Dad, it was just a dream," Jason said.

"Right. Yeah, you're right. Just a dream." Michael said as he got back on the road. Jason was a little freaked out. His dad was acting worried, which wasn't a good sign for a so-called dream. After a very long, quiet ride, they pulled up at his school and parked. "If you have any more dreams make sure to tell me ok. It's ok to talk to me again. I love you, son, and it will all make sense soon enough." Michael said. Jason turned and looked at his father before getting out of the car. What his dad said bothered him because his mother had said the same thing in his dream. He was starting to think it wasn't a dream after all.

He got out of the car and texted Ava. "Meet me in the gym locker room hallway at your school."

"Alright, I'm on my way," Ava replied. He then ran into school to find a place to be alone so people wouldn't see his powers. As soon as he walked in, he ran into Sky.

"Hey, I was wondering if you were coming today. You missed yesterday." Sky said.

"Oh yeah. Sorry about that. My grandma and my dad took me birthday shopping," Jason said. He saw Henry walking toward him. "Can I talk to you at lunch, Sky? Sorry, I just have something to do." Jason said as he walked away. Sky watched as he ran up to Henry and ran down the hall out of sight. Jason and Henry ran to the boy's bathroom to get away from everyone. Jason ran around checking the stalls to make sure they were alone.

"What are you doing, and what's this plan you were talking about?" Henry asked.

"Give me your hands," Jason said. Henry held out his hands and then stopped and jerked them back really fast.

"Wait! Why? Oh no, you are not about to try what I think you are?" Henry asked.

"Just give me your hands, Henry! Before someone walks in!" Jason said. Henry squinched his eyes and held his hands out, and

Jason grabbed them and told Henry not to let go. He then thought of the hallway in front of the locker rooms in Ava's school. He opened his eyes, and they were there. "Henry, you can open your eyes now," Jason said. As soon as he opened his eyes he ran to the trash can in the hall and threw up.

"Why does my stomach feel so weird?" Henry asked.

"It goes away don't worry about it," Jason said.

"So you have done this before?" Henry asked another question.

"Once, but it was just to my bathroom," Jason said.

"Wait, what are we doing at Ava's school?" Henry asked. Just at that time, Ava finally ran around the corner. "Hey guys, I'm here," Ava said.

"Ava knows now?" Henry asked.

"Yes." Jason nodded.

"So, how are we going to get to Henry's?" Ava asked very slowly. Jason looked at Henry and smiled.

"Oh God, No, can't we just walk?" Henry asked.

"Sure, and they are just going to let us walk right out of school? Everyone hold hands and close your eyes, and whatever happens, don't let go." Jason said. He then thought of Henry's attic. After a few seconds, he opened his eyes and was very surprised. They were there. "You can open your eyes now," Jason said. Henry sat down on the floor.

"I think I'm going to be sick again," Henry said.

"That was so awesome," Ava said. She began to walk around the attic while Jason sat with Henry for a minute.

"When did Ava find out about you?" Henry asked.

"I was trying to tell you this morning. She woke me up from my dream last night, and I accidentally threw her." Jason said.

"You threw her? Did she get hurt?" Henry asked in a very concerned voice. Jason just smiled and patted Henry's shoulder and then stood up.

"Ok, so where are these things I need to see?" Jason asked.

"They are over here. They are pictures of your mom. Can you handle looking at these?" Henry asked as he stood up and walked over to the pictures.

"Yes, I have to figure this out," Jason said. He started going through the pictures, and one of them was his mom standing on top of a bucket that was sitting on top of the water, and Henry's mom was there. The next picture was both their moms again. Jason's mom had her hand above a glass, and Henry's mom had her hand sitting under the cup on the table. The glass was floating, and they were both laughing. '*What did these pictures mean?*' Jason thought. "Look what I found," Jason said.

"Is that both our moms?" Henry asked.

"Let me see," Ava said while taking pictures from Jason.

"This has to mean something, right? My mom used powers? You can see it in the picture. So maybe your mom knows about my mom." Jason said as he looked at Henry.

"It's possible, but there has to be someone else who knows, too," Henry said.

"What do you mean?" Ava asked.

"The person taking the picture; who do you think it was?" Henry asked.

Thirty minutes had passed, and Jason didn't want to stop looking through everything. "We have to get back to school. We can look again this weekend. My mom has to work." Henry said. Jason put the pictures he had found in his pocket, and they all got together and grabbed hands. After dropping Ava back off at school and finally returning to their own school, Jason was trying to decide if he should give the pictures to his grandma and ask her what they meant. The boys both had Algebra that morning, so they were sitting in class together when Jason had a daydream. It was another dream about his mom. He was sitting there doing his math work when someone walked up and sat on the corner of his desk. "Jason, you have to tell your grandma that you have received your gifts," Emma said.

"How are you even here? Are you really here?" Jason asked.

"I'm in your head, but yes, this is real," Emma replied.

"I don't understand. Are you a ghost?" Jason asked.

"Something like that, but that's not what is important right now. You need to go home and talk to your grandma. She will explain everything to you." Emma said.

"I almost hurt Ava, Mom," Jason said.

"I know I have been watching, and you are only going to get stronger. If you don't learn to control your powers, Jason, you will kill someone." Emma said. There was a sudden loud noise that made him jump. As he looked up, his teacher was standing there with Jason's book. He had picked it up and slammed it on his desk.

"Well, thank you for joining us again, Jason." Mr. Hicks said. As Hicks walked away, Jason turned and looked at Henry, and he was trying to tell Henry that he had a daydream about his mom, but Henry couldn't hear him or read his lips. All of a sudden, Henry screamed and jumped up and fell to the floor, holding his head. "Stop... Just stop!" Henry yelled.

Jason jumped up and grabbed him. "Are you ok? Henry, open your eyes. Look at me, Henry," Jason said in a terrified voice.

"Jason, move back!" Mr. Hicks yelled. As he stepped back, all he could think about was Henry hurting, and then, all of a sudden, he stopped screaming. "Are you ok, Henry?" Mr. Hicks asked. "I think so," Henry answered.

"Jason, take your friend here to the nurse. He needs to be checked out," Mr. Hicks said.

As they left the room, Henry looked at Jason and asked. "Why did you do that?"

"Do what?" Jason asked.

"You started yelling at me in my mind. It hurt so bad." Henry said.

"I didn't know I could get in people's heads. I mean, it was just a thought. I was thinking, I wish I could just tell you without actually saying it." Jason said.

"Well, you did, Jason. You definitely told me. I heard you loud and clear. Now the question is, are you going to tell your grandma?" Henry asked. Jason just looked down the hallway in a blank stare because he didn't know if he was ready to tell anyone. All he knew was his mom had the answers and he was starting to think something bad happened to her.

It was now lunch time and Henry had a checkup with the nurse and told her it was just a headache and he was good to go. The boys went to the lunch room and sat at their table with their food. Sky and Mya decided to join them. "So tomorrow is party day," Sky started the conversation. "What time do you want us there?"

"The party starts at 6, but you can come early if you want, and we will have some time to talk before the party gets busy," Jason said.

"What about you, Henry?" Mya asked.

"Yeah, I will be there. I'm staying over there tonight, so I can be there all day tomorrow to help set up." Henry answered.

"Give me your phone, Jason," Sky said with a smile. He handed her his phone and sat there while she scrolled through it, and even though he wasn't sure what she was doing, he couldn't say anything. He has loved this girl forever. She then smiled and handed him his phone back, and then her phone beeped. "I added my number and sent myself a text so that I could have yours. Now, the next time you can't be at school you can at least let me know you're ok." Sky said with a smile, then leaned in and kissed him on the cheek. As she leaned in and kissed him, someone grabbed her and pulled her away. Sky turned around, and it was her brother Mike.

"What are you doing, Sky? I think you should sit with me." Mike said.

"I'm fine where I am, Mike. I'm sitting with my boyfriend, Jason." Sky said. Jason looked at her and smiled. He didn't say it, but he loved hearing her call him her boyfriend. Mike then gave Jason a look that, in a way, seemed like he wanted to hurt him as he walked to his own table. "Don't worry about my brother. I can handle him." Sky said to Jason. They all sit together through the lunch period, talking about the party. After a long day, it was finally time to go home. When he walked over to Ava's school, he saw his father parked there.

"What are you doing here, Dad?" Jason asked.

"I'm here to pick you and Ava up," Michael replied.

"I always meet Ava close to the door," Jason said.

"That's fine. I will be right here waiting." Michael said. He walked up to the spot where he and Ava always meet, and before he could even sit, she walked out. They talked on the way back to the car about his dream and what he should do. "I think you should tell grandma," Ava said.

"I honestly want to. I think the powers might have come from Mom, and if they did, Grandma should know about them. Just don't say anything in front of dad." Jason said as they walked up to the car. After a long, quiet car ride home, they pulled into the driveway and saw the front door to the house was open. "Did you leave that open dad?" Jason asked.

"No, I didn't. I'm honestly not sure why it would be open because I locked it." Michael said. They all got out and ran to the house. Ava was the first in, and as she ran in, she saw a man chasing Evelyn and screamed, "Jason!" He had just run in behind her and seen the whole thing. He yelled, "Hey!" and quickly waved his hand and threw the man through the window behind him. He then looked at his grandma, who was looking behind him. When he turned around, his dad was standing there. "It's time for that talk," Michael said.

They were all sitting in the family room, but everyone was quiet. Jason had many questions to ask but didn't know where to start. One question was why wasn't anyone surprised or freaking out over what he did. He stood up and took the pictures out of his pocket and threw them on the coffee table. "Since no one else is going to talk, I will just ask a question. What are these and do they have to do with what's going on with me?" Jason asked.

"Where did you get those?" Evelyn asked as she picked them up. "Henry's, he has more than this in their attic. I want to know what they mean," Jason said. Evelyn looked at Michael. "Ok, Jason, you deserve to know everything. You have already received your powers, so it's time – You are a warlock. Your mom was a witch as well as I. We had to wait till you received your powers before we could tell you." Evelyn said.

"I am also a warlock. Your mom and I met at school. We felt each other's powers and were drawn to each other. After a year, possibly sooner, you will begin to feel others around you with power or anything from the supernatural." Michael said.

"Anything supernatural? I just found out witches are real. Now you're telling me other things are out there as well?" Jason asked.

"Yes. I know this is a lot to take in at once." Michael said.

"Really, you know it's a lot; what am I supposed to say to all this?" Jason asked.

"There is more," Evelyn said, interrupting Jason and his father. Jason looked at her with a confused look.

"What more could there be?" Jason asked.

"You came from both supernatural parents. Most kids only have one supernatural parent. Since you have two, you will be very powerful. You won't need spells like most witches and warlocks.

You will be able to conjure things by just a simple thought," Evelyn said.

"Yeah, Grandma, you are a little late for that. Jason can already do that," Ava said. Michael and Evelyn looked at Ava and then at Jason. "Just how much can you do, Jason?" Evelyn asked.

"More than you, apparently, since I had to save you," Jason said in a sarcastic, aggravated voice.

"I think you need to calm down," Michael said.

"Just show us something you can do," Evelyn said.

Ava jumped up and asked. "Let's show her. Can we, Jason?"

He smiled because he knew what she wanted to do. He walked up to her and whispered to her. "I'm going to send you to the kitchen, and I want you to grab an apple, and then I'm going to bring you back," Jason said. She started laughing and was very excited. She loved travelling.

"Close your eyes, Ava," Jason said. As she closed her eyes, he held out both hands in front of him and she disappeared. Michael jumped up from the chair. "What did you do? Where is your sister?" Michael asked in a concerned voice.

"Sit down, Dad. I'm not done," Jason said. He then held his hands out again, and she reappeared with the apple and tossed it to Evelyn.

"That was so much fun. Can we do it again?" Ava asked.

"Just wait, Ava. Ok, so you can throw people obviously and travel objects and people." Michael said.

"I can do more than that, Dad," Jason said. Evelyn stood up at this point.

"He shouldn't have that much power yet, should he?" Evelyn asked in a perplexed and concerned voice.

"I don't know. I have never met anyone that had both supernatural parents, but we have heard they are the most powerful of all," Michael said.

"I guess we are seeing it firsthand," Evelyn said as she looked at Jason with a worried look.

They all stood there quietly for a few minutes before Jason decided it was time for some answers. "So what are the dreams with mom about?" Jason asked.

Evelyn sat down slowly and grabbed her locket that was hanging from her neck and then looked at Jason and Ava.

"I know you both grew up with the idea your mom was dead, but do either of you actually remember a funeral?" Michael asked. Jason looked at Ava.

"Wait, are you saying our mom is alive?" Jason asked.

"Yes. She was taken by a witch hunter and placed in a special place that she can't leave unless she is released with a key. It's not just a normal key. It's an artifact I have spent all these years searching for," Michael said.

"That's where you have been? Trying to save mom?" Ava asked.

"Yes, and I couldn't take you two with me. It was just too dangerous for you." Michael replied.

"So you just kept it from us? You couldn't say she went to live somewhere else? We thought she was dead. There was a better way to handle that, Dad," Jason said in an angry voice. "How about we all take a break? I'm hungry, and I'm sure everyone else is, too," Evelyn interrupted. She decided they should eat pizza since it was fast, and they apparently were going to be talking for a while. "I'm going to order pizza. What does everyone want?" Evelyn asked.

"Just let Jason take care of it, Grandma," Ava said. He looked at Ava and smiled. He loved his sister, and he loved that she had been by his side with full confidence since she found out about him. He walked to the kitchen, and with a wave of his hand, the table was set and full of pizza. Ava ran to her seat and started eating. "He has done the same thing to my backpack," Ava said. You could tell Michael had a lot on his mind, but he didn't say anything. They all just sat down to eat when they heard a knock at the door.

"I got it," Jason said. He opened the door, and it was Henry.

"Hey, can we talk outside? It's about this morning and what happened when I got off the bus," Henry said.

"You can just come to the kitchen," Jason said.

"No, I can't talk about this in front of everyone," Henry said.

"They know," Jason said.

"They know what?" Henry asked.

"Everything," Jason said.

"How do they know? Did you tell them?" Henry asked.

"Not exactly; when we got home today, there was a man in the house trying to hurt grandma, so I threw him out the window, and well, they saw everything," Jason said.

"Did they freak out?" Henry asked.

"No. It was actually the opposite," Jason replied. He gave Jason a perplexed look.

"Just come eat with us. We have pizza, and I will explain," Jason said. So Henry joined them in the kitchen. Jason told him everything and that the gift runs in the family.

"So the guy that attacked your grandma was trying to kill her?" Henry asked.

"I believe so," Jason said.

"So I wonder if this was the same guy," Henry said as he threw a picture on the table.

"What do you mean, same guy?" Jason asked as he picked it up.

"When I got off the bus some guy was parked across the road and watched me walk inside. I took a picture." Henry said.

"It's the hunter. We should cancel the party," Michael said.

"No the only thing that will do is tell the hunter we are on to him and know who he is. He needs to think we don't know what he is. Besides, he won't do anything in front of all the people that will be here." Evelyn said.

"But why are they watching Henry's house?" Jason asked.

"How long has Henry known about you?" Michael asked.

"Since I found out I have powers that I had to figure out on my own. You would think that you or grandma would have told me. Why didn't you?" Jason asked.

"We didn't want to chance you telling anyone and being found before you could protect yourself. Please don't be mad. We were only doing what we thought was best," Evelyn said.

"Well, that worked out great. I ended up saving you. What would you have done if we hadn't come home when we did? You would be dead right." Jason said.

"Jason! I think we should just take a break. This is too much at once." Michael said. Jason looked at his dad with an aggravated look and then walked away. He couldn't believe they kept this from him all these years.

Jason decided to go upstairs with Henry and talk about everything. When the boys got to Jason's room, they heard Evelyn and Michael talking. "He is very powerful. To conjure a full table of food and not feel weak; I mean, we knew he would be different, but this is more than anyone could have ever imagined." Michael said.

"What will we do if it consumes him? We have both heard the stories. Some turn bad when they have too much power. What will we do? We need to tell him," Evelyn said. Michael just kept looking at the glass in front of him at the table. She could tell he was in deep thought.

"Are you listening to me, Michael?" Evelyn asked in a strong voice.

"I'm sorry, yes I heard you. I wonder if he could conjure the artifact we need to release Emma. If he could, we would be one step closer to getting her back. We would only have to find the door," Michael said. At that moment, Jason came running downstairs, followed by Henry.

"You're saying I could save mom?" Jason asked. They both looked at him.

"How much did you hear, Jason?" Evelyn asked.

"I heard everything. It's not going to change me. I'm stronger than you think," Jason continued. "Now, what does the artifact look like?"

At that moment, Ava came in from the living room. "There is a letter outside. I didn't see who brought it." Ava said.

"Why were you outside? You could have been killed." Henry said in an aggravated voice.

"I thought I heard someone at the door, so I checked," Ava said as she walked away. Jason went to the door and grabbed the letter and he gave it to Evelyn. After carefully opening it, she read it slowly. It was from the Hunter. He said he knew about Jason and what he was and that he would be watching him closely. She showed the letter to Michael, who in return showed it to Jason and Henry. Jason used his mind to tell Henry to take Ava upstairs. "Go upstairs with Henry Ava," Jason said.

"What does it say?" Ava said.

"Just go," Jason said as Henry grabbed her hand. She looked at Henry and followed him. As she went upstairs, Jason looked at Michael and then at Evelyn with a worried look. "What are we going to do if he goes after Ava? Would he do that to try and get to me?" Jason asked.

"That's not something I can answer. It depends on the hunter. Some of them are different and have little humanity left, while others let their aggression toward witches take them over. In other words, he could take her, yes, and depending on how much he hates us, he could kill her." Michael said.

"Well, I'm not going to let that happen. Ava is the one person out of this mess that can't defend herself. We have to protect her." Jason said. "I know this is going to sound crazy, but keep her close to Henry. It doesn't make sense yet but trust that she will be safe. She will not be hurt with him around," Evelyn said.

"Yeah let's just leave her in the hands of a human against the witch hunter. That's not crazy at all!" Jason yelled.

"It will make sense later, I promise," Evelyn said.

As he headed up the stairs, he found Ava halfway up. She had been sitting there listening to everything. "Am I going to die, Jason?" Ava asked as she cried. Henry was beside her and grabbed her and wrapped her into a tight hug.

"No, you're not going to die, Ava. I won't let anyone hurt you," Henry said. Jason gave Henry a look that was different than what he expected. It was more like a thank-you look. Henry walked her to her room and decided to lay with her for a few minutes until she fell asleep. He came out of her room, and Jason was standing there. He thought Jason might throw him or try to hurt him again, so he began groveling. "Look, I'm really sorry. I don't know why they thought she would be safe with me or why she was clinging to me. I just know I care about her, and I don't want her to get hurt, so whatever you have planned, I'm in." Henry said while backing up against the wall, watching Jason. Jason held his hand out to shake Henry's hand. He was surprised, but he stepped forward and shook Jason's hand in agreement.

"So you do have a thing for my sister?" Jason asked in a sarcastic, joking way.

"Shut up, man," Henry said. They laughed as they walked into Jason's room. The boys sat down and started talking about Jason's mom and how he might be able to get the key to release his mom from wherever she was. Jason still wasn't sure about that answer. He just knew she was alive, and he needed to save her. They also talked about Henry and why they seemed so ok with him knowing everything. It was as if they thought he belonged. "What if I'm like an amazing wizard or something," Henry said while laughing.

"Come on, man, be for real. We need to figure out what everyone is hiding from us and why," Jason said.

"Well, I know it's something that my mom has to know, right? Why else would she have those pictures?" Henry asked.

"Let's get some sleep and figure this out tomorrow," Jason said. He was also worried about what Sky would think if she knew what he was.

Sky was at home with Mya, talking about Jason and Henry. They were very excited about the party and talked about what they would wear.

"Nothing, because you're not going," Mike said as he walked around the corner.

"Is that right…and you're going to stop me?" Sky asked with a very sarcastic voice.

"What would Mom say, Sky? You don't need to be dating him. You are putting the whole family out there by doing so," Mike said.

"I can handle myself, Mike and so can Mya. We know what we are doing," Sky replied. Mya was just looking at the corner of the bed, scared to speak.

"Yeah, just sit there and be her little follower, Mya…you know this is wrong," Mike said.

"Leave her alone…just because you can't find someone to put up with you doesn't mean everyone else has to be miserable like you," Sky said.

"I can find a date…don't worry about that, and you will all love who it will be. The party is going to be totally fun I will make sure of that," Mike said.

"Don't you ruin the party, Mike? Why would you even want to go? It's not even your thing," Sky said.

"Oh, you know, to have fun, be a teenager, and of course you can't forget about eating. There will be lots to eat there," Mike said with a mean voice.

"Don't you dare Mike? I'm not kidding. I will make you regret it," Sky said.

"See you two at the party," Mike said as he walked out of the room smiling.

"Don't worry, Sky…he wouldn't dare. Your mom would be mad if he acted out at the party," Mya said. They both decided to lie down after the drama was over and tried to sleep before the party day.

CHAPTER 4

The morning of the party only one person was up. It was Ava. She was making Jason's birthday breakfast like she does every year. See, Jason wasn't big on celebrating his birthday, but he loved spending it with her, so she wasn't missing this year either. She made a big breakfast for everyone. Just as she was about to set the table, Henry headed down stairs. "What are you doing?" Henry asked.

"Making Jason's birthday breakfast; I do this every year the first weekend after his birthday. It's a routine, and he loves it," Ava said.

"Do you want some help?" Henry asked.

"You can help set the table if you want," Ava replied. He started grabbing plates and cups to set out on the table. Just as he set everything out, he ran into Ava, and she was carrying the juice pitcher. She dropped it, and he quickly caught it. "Nice reflexes,"

Ava said as she smiled. He smiled back, and the two couldn't stop looking at each other.

"So, do I get breakfast or what?" Jason said from the doorway. She jumped and looked at the door and he was standing with his arms and feet crossed and propped up against the door frame.

"Jason!" Ava yelled. "You scared me. Don't do that." He laughed and walked by and raised his eyebrows at Henry and then winked at him.

"Not funny, man," Henry said. They sat down and started eating. Soon, Evelyn walked in, followed by Michael. They handed Jason 4 pictures. "One of these has to be the key to letting your mom out. We need them all, and then, hopefully, I will be able to feel the power from the correct one." Michael said. Jason stood up and took the pictures to the living room.

One was a dragon, one was a tiger, one was a dog, and the other was a lion. "I don't need to get them all. I have seen it in my dreams with Mom. It was always in the background, and I didn't think anything about it, but it looks just like this," Jason said as he held up the picture of the tiger. Jason looked at the picture again, and he knew it would be the most powerful thing he had done since he received his powers, but it was for his mom. Michael stayed close by him, waiting for the artifact to appear. Jason sat down in the chair, closed his eyes, took a few deep breaths, and then pictured the tiger in his hand. The lights started flickering, and there was a slight breeze as if his power was flowing around the room. Everyone was watching him and looking around the room as they were very scared.

It was strange enough to make Michael step back. At that moment, the tiger appeared in Jason's hand. It was very beautiful, and after Jason set it down on the table he looked at Michael. "Well, that was new," Ava said. They turned to see her watching. "That didn't happen when we made my backpack appear."

"He had to bring this a lot further than just a few rooms, so it took more power," Evelyn said.

"Let's go get Mom," Jason said as he jumped to his feet.

"We will, but I still have to find the door, and we need to get rid of the hunter. If he finds out what we are doing, he will put us with your mom." Michael said. Everyone got quiet for a minute, and Jason knew he couldn't just go get his mom. Things have been hard on him, being like a father to Ava, thinking his mom was dead, and now finding out she is alive and held prisoner somewhere. It was just a lot to take in for only being 16.

Evelyn was thinking about how to end the silence and get everyone's mind off of the bad things for a while, but first, she had to get everyone moving. "Alright, how about we eat this lovely breakfast before it gets too cold? Ava, you did a lovely job," Evelyn said. Everyone went to the kitchen to eat, and everything started to seem normal. Jason was smiling. He didn't have to hide anything from anyone in the room. He could just be himself, and he loved it. He was even bonding with his father for once, talking about the funny things that happened with his powers, like throwing Henry over the loft railing in the barn. "Well, it's party day, and we need to finish the barn. Boys, you need to go to the store," Evelyn said.

"Boys? I'm included in this, am I?" Michael asked while laughing.

"Yes, you are, and I don't want to hear any complaining," Evelyn said with a smile while smacking Michael on the arm with a towel.

"Well, you heard her boys. Let's go," Michael said.

"I will text you a list of the food to get," Evelyn said.

Michael led Jason and Henry outside. "I have a great idea. Why don't we let Jason drive?" Michael asked.

"Really, Dad, you're going to let me drive?" Jason asked.

"Yeah, why not? You have a license now." Michael said.

He grabbed the keys and jumped in the driver's seat. "Can Henry take a shotgun, Dad?" Jason asked.

Michael just smiled and got in the back, and Henry ran to the passenger side. They headed to town. Jason looked in the mirror and saw Michael on his phone. After pulling into the store, he tried to hand the keys back to Michael. "Boys, I will be right back. I have to go across the street for a second. I sent the list to your phone, Jason. Hold onto the keys till I get back. Here is the money for the food. I will be right back." Michael said.

Jason and Henry headed into the store. They went over the list, and it was a bunch of little things. They went around slowly collecting everything and talking about the party until Henry grabbed Jason. "Look, it's Sky. Go say hi, man."

"She will be at the party later. Why don't I just wait till then?" Jason asked.

"Really, just go say hi," Henry said. He gave Henry a look but he decided it couldn't hurt to bump into someone at the store casually. They took the same isle she did and found she was with Mya as well. As they walked closer, they bumped their buggy into theirs. "I'm sorry we didn't see you," Henry said.

Sky and Mya smiled. "So the party is tonight. What are the plans?" Sky asked.

"My grandma is letting us have the party in the loft of the barn so we can all be alone but also close enough for her or my dad to bust us for having too much fun," Jason said while laughing. Sky and Mya both laughed.

"What time do you want us there?" Mya asked.

"The party starts at six, but you are welcome to come over whenever you are ready. We could maybe go for a horse ride before the party. Well, if you want to?" Jason asked.

"Sounds like fun," Sky said as she walked by.

"See you guys later," Mya said.

The boys finished their shopping and went out to the car and Michael wasn't there. "Where is my dad? He said he would be right back, right?" Jason asked.

"Yeah, that's what I heard. Let's just load everything in the car and give him a few more minutes." Henry said.

After the boys finished putting everything in the car, Jason received a text from Michael. "Go ahead and head to the house. I will have your grandma come get me. This is taking longer than I thought." He showed the text to Henry.

"Well, I guess let's head back to your house," Henry said.

The boys talked about things on the way home, about all the crazy things that have happened. "So much for being normal, I guess," Jason said.

"I know. It's almost like everything in our lives has been a lie," Henry said.

"I feel like it's going to get a lot crazier before we figure things out," Jason agreed. Henry just looked at Jason. It was almost as if Henry was saying I'm right here with you till the end. Jason pulled up at the farm and saw a truck he had never seen before. "Henry, I don't know that truck. Ava and Grandma are alone in there." Jason said in a worried voice. The boys ran to the house, shoved the door open, and ran inside, only to see everyone in the living room, including Jason's father.

"These are yours, Jason," Michael said as he handed Jason a set of keys.

"What are they?" Jason asked.

"Oh my God, man. That truck, it's yours," Henry said with excitement. "You guys scared us. We thought someone we didn't know was here, so we were coming to fight."

"I'm sorry, sweetie. We didn't mean to scare you," Evelyn said.

"Well, go on. Out of all the bad going on, it's time for some fun. Happy birthday, son." Michael said. Henry took off running outside. Honestly, he seemed more excited than Jason. Ava ran out behind Henry, followed by Jason, Michael, and Evelyn. Jason got in the truck and asked everyone if they wanted to go for a ride. Henry and Ava jumped in the truck, of course. "We will take the next ride. Have fun and be safe, ok." Evelyn said.

Jason loved his new truck. It was a huge four-door black truck with four-wheel drive. What else could a 16-year-old boy ask for? He drove them all into town with Ava in the back seat and Henry riding shotgun. "Who wants ice cream?" Jason asked.

"Sure, but I'm buying. It's your birthday." Henry said. "Technically, my birthday was three days ago," Jason said sarcastically. Ava started laughing in the back seat. While the kids were off having fun, Evelyn and Michael started setting up for the party. Michael made the food while Evelyn wrapped presents. It was very quiet for a while.

"So, do you think they will come back?" Michael asked sarcastically. Evelyn looked at Michael.

"Not a chance," Evelyn said while laughing.

"I know you are upset with me because I left the kids for so long, but I only did it trying to get Emma back for the kids," Michael said.

"I'm not upset with you. I am glad you found a way to get her back. I miss my daughter. I just wish the kids didn't have to feel the pain of our mistakes," Evelyn replied. At that moment, they heard the truck pull in. They all came in laughing. "What's so funny?" Evelyn asked.

"We went and got ice cream," Ava said.

Evelyn gave them a look. "Ok, Grandma, I let Henry and Ava stand up through the sunroof, but I was going slowly," Jason said.

Evelyn started laughing. "The look works every time."

It was an hour before the party when a little red car pulled up. Ava looked out the window and said, "Two girls are here,"

Henry looked at Jason. "They are here," Henry said. Jason walked outside, followed by Henry. Ava watched as they walked out and hugged the girls.

"So you decided to come early. Does that mean you want to go on that horse ride?" Jason asked.

"Well, instead of a ride, how about we just go see the horses in the barn? I don't want to get dirty before the party," Sky asked. As they walked to the barn, Ava ran to her room. It was time to start getting ready. She went through her closet and couldn't find anything she wanted to wear. After sitting in her room sad for a minute, she thought about her mom's old dresses from school. They were in her grandma's closet. She ran to Evelyn's room and started going through the dresses and finally found a beautiful blue dress that was tight with a hanging blue silk see-through slip that fell over it and was attached on top of the shoulders with a cut out back. "*This is perfect,*" Ava thought to herself. She quickly went back to her room to get ready.

Back in the barn the boys were showing the girls around. Letting them meet all the horses. "So, where is your brother tonight?" Jason asked.

"I don't know. I told him he was a Jerk and to leave me alone and that whoever I decided to date was none of his business." Sky said.

"I bet he loved hearing that. He probably hates me even more now," Jason said with a little laugh.

"Does it matter? I like you, which should be all that matters," Sky said as she started to lean in to kiss Jason.

"So, are you girls hungry?" Evelyn interrupted their romance even before it started. "We are about to bring the food out here to the barn."

Jason turned around and saw both Evelyn and Michael standing there and smiled. He knew Grandma wouldn't leave them alone too long. "Actually, yes, I'm starving. Let us help with the food." Sky said.

Evelyn looked at Jason with a look that said I like this girl. Evelyn took the girls back to the house as Michael stayed behind to talk to the boys. "OK, you two. I expect you both to be gentlemen tonight."

"Yes, sir." Jason and Henry said. As everyone started showing up, Evelyn began to get the cake ready. As she was putting the candles on the cake, Ava started coming down the stairs and walked into the kitchen. At first, she thought she was looking at Emma. Ava looked just like her mother. With the same dress, heels, and hairstyle as Emma, she could be her twin. Her hair was a great length and it was twirled into a messy bun with curls coming out almost like a flower and then the tail of her hair hanging down to her left side with curls. Evelyn started crying a little as she told Ava how beautiful she was. "You look just like your mother. She would be so happy with the little woman you are becoming, Ava." Ava smiled and hugged Evelyn. "I will see you out there, Grandma," Ava said as she walked to the door.

As Ava walked to the barn, she ran into a boy. "I'm so sorry. I was looking at my phone and didn't see you. My name is Ava. I'm Jason's little sister." Ava said.

"No, it's alright. No bruises. So why is a girl like you walking to the party alone?" The boy asked.

"I don't have a date. It's just me," Ava said with a smile.

"Well, we can't have a beautiful girl like you escorting herself. My name is Mike. Would you like a date for this party?" Mike asked.

"I would love a date," Ava answered. She didn't know Mike was Sky's brother, who didn't like Jason because he was dating Sky. The two made their way to the barn and slowly walked up the stairs. As they got close to the top of the stairs, Mike wrapped his arm around Ava's waist and nudged her closer. She thought it was sweet, so she smiled. At that moment, Jason and Henry saw Ava with Mike.

"Your brother is with my sister Sky. Will he hurt her because he's mad at me?" Jason asked with a straight face. "No, he wouldn't dare hurt her. He just wants it to bug you. Just ignore him. He just wants to get in your head because I'm dating you," Sky replied.

"How about we go over and talk to him," Henry said.

"No, don't. He will hurt both of you," Sky said. Jason and Henry laughed a little.

"Apparently, you don't know my boy Jason," Henry said.

"Please, I'm begging you. Let it go, Jason. He won't hurt her, I promise," Sky pleaded.

Jason looked at Sky, and he could tell she was really scared, so he decided to leave it alone as long as Ava seemed happy. "Do you want to dance?" Jason asked.

"I would love to dance with you, Jason," Sky was relieved.

Henry and Mya kept sitting in the corner where they could see the whole dance floor and Henry kept watching Ava. He refused to take his eyes off her. Mya finally realized that she wasn't who Henry wanted to be there with. "Henry, I need to tell you something. I said yes that I would come with you to the party but we can only be friends. I actually have a boyfriend. He just lives somewhere else at the moment," Mya said.

Henry turned to Mya. "I understand. I just didn't want to come alone to the party." They both started laughing.

Jason and Sky headed back to their seats when the song was over. "So you're both having fun without us?" Jason said sarcastically as he was walking up to his seat with Sky which took Henry's attention back to the dance floor. That's when Henry realized Ava was gone.

"Jason, she is gone," Henry said.

"Who, Henry?" Jason asked.

"Ava!" Henry yelled. The boys jumped up and started looking for her around the room. They went down the stairs looking in the barn and finally went outside looking for her. The girls finally came out and started helping them look. After a few minutes, someone started screaming. They ran around the side of the barn, and there was Ava and Mike. They were standing by a person lying on the ground, and Ava was crying into Mike's shoulder.

"What happened?" Jason asked. Ava turned to see Jason and Henry standing there, and she ran to Henry and he quickly wrapped his arms around her and turned towards the house. "I'm taking Ava to the house."

As Ava and Henry walked into the house Evelyn saw Ava had been crying and ran to her. "What's wrong, Ava? Are you ok?" Evelyn asked.

"The better question would be, whose blood is that?" Michael asked as he looked at her shoes. Ava looked down to see she had been standing in blood, and it was all over her shoes. She began to scream, trying to get her shoes off. Henry put his hands on Ava's face so she would look at him. "Calm down, Ava, and sit down. I will help you. It's going to be ok." Henry said in a very calm voice. He was freaking out, too but trying to stay calm for Ava because he knew if he panicked, it would make Ava even more scared.

Jason decided to take a closer look at the body to see if she was dead. There was so much blood he was sure she was dead. As Jason grabbed her hand to check for a pulse, she moved, opened her eyes, and then started screaming and crying while slapping at everyone who came near her. "Dad!" Jason yelled! Michael was already headed to the barn after seeing the blood on Ava's shoes, and he heard Jason yelling his name and ran to him.

As he came up behind Jason, he saw the girl lying there. "Looks like she cut herself. Everyone, go back to the party. Jason, help me get her to the house so we can get help for her," Michael said. "Calm down, and let us help you. We are going to take you to the house and call your parents."

Jason and Michael helped her up and helped her walk to the house. As they got close to the house, Jason thought about Ava. She will freak out if she sees this girl covered in blood again. "Henry, take Ava to her room!" Jason yelled!

Henry heard Jason just in time to get Ava upstairs. "Why do we have to come up here?" Ava asked.

"I'm not sure, but I won't leave you. I will turn away so you can change if you want to get out of that dress. Just tell me what you want to do," Henry said. He was trying to make her more comfortable so that she wouldn't be so scared.

"That's ok. I can change in my closet," Ava replied. As Ava went into the closet to change, Henry walked around the room, looking at all her things and then went to look out the window. Ava's bedroom window faced the barn. He was making sure everything was ok while they were all in the house. "Thank you, Henry, for taking care of me," Ava said. Henry turned around and Ava was right behind him.

"I told you I would protect you. I'm not going anywhere," Henry said. "Do you want to watch a movie while we wait for Jason to call us downstairs?" Henry asked. Ava just smiled and then set on the bed and stared at the floor.

"Our lives will never be the same again, will it?" Ava questioned. Henry walked over to the bed and stood in front of Ava.

He brushed her hair back with his hand and then hugged her. "I promise everything will be fine. I will stay as long as you need me to," Henry said as he held her. Ava stood up, and Henry stepped back to give her some space. Ava turned and walked around the bed and sat down.

"What movie are we going to watch?" Ava asked. Henry picked out a movie and sat down with her. "Can I lie on your shoulder, Henry?" Ava asked. He slowly leaned back against the headboard and looked at her. She leaned in, laid her head down, and started watching the movie. He could tell she was still upset about earlier and wanted to comfort her.

Jason and Michael were downstairs trying to get the girl to stop bleeding and crying so they could ask her what happened. Evelyn ran in from the kitchen with a towel, cold water, and ice. She dipped the towel in cold water and then wrapped it in ice. "This will slow down the bleeding and the ambulance is on their way. Who should we call for you?" Evelyn asked.

The girl handed Evelyn her phone. "What happened to your neck?" Jason asked. The girl started crying again. "No one is going to hurt you anymore, I promise. I won't let anyone get to you, but I need you to tell me what happened." Jason said.

"He bit me" were the only words she said. Jason looked at Michael with confusion. "He bit her? Who bit her and why?" Jason asked.

"Hold this on her neck, Jason. I need to talk to your father," Evelyn said. Evelyn and Michael ran into the kitchen.

"Are you thinking what I am?" Evelyn asked.

"Yes, but this is insane. They have been gone from this area for years. They can't be back, can they?" Michael asked.

"Well, let's think. Emma placed the ban on the town, and she is in a type of spiritual prison. With her being gone and not able to since them, we don't really know if they are back. So yeah, I guess it's possible," Evelyn said.

"These might not be the same ones, though. After all, they left her alive; the others wouldn't have done that unless they were stopped or scared away." Michael said. Jason was tired of being left out, so he was going to figure this out. He slowly removed the towel to see what the bite looked like, and he could swear it was a vampire bite. It was a bunch of little holes but four big ones, two on top and two on bottom. He put the towel back and didn't say a word. He just looked at her and smiled so she wouldn't worry. Evelyn and Michael were still in the kitchen when they heard the sirens of the ambulance. Evelyn grabbed the girl's phone and called her mom to tell her what happened and what hospital they were going to send her to. Michael joined Jason in the living room. "Let's get her ready, Jason. Your mom is coming to the hospital to meet you. You're going to be ok." Michael said.

As the ambulance left, Jason turned to Michael and Evelyn. "It was a vampire, wasn't it?" Jason asked.

"We don't know," Evelyn replied.

"No! No, you're not going to do that. I deserve to know the truth. I have some crazy powers. I have stopped a hunter from killing you, Grandma, and I handled it all very well. Now tell me, it is a vampire, isn't it?" Jason asked.

"Okay, look, son, we honestly don't know. We think it could be, but we can't be sure. They were not supposed to be able to enter our town because your mom had a spell cast on the town and would since any supernatural that walked into town. She had problems with a vampire family a few years after we were together. One of the boys liked your mother, and she chose me. He wasn't happy," Michael answered.

"But mom is gone now; does that mean they can get in without us knowing?" Jason asked another question.

"That's what we need to figure out, and it's not like any of us know a vampire to ask," Evelyn replied.

"Great, so now we have a hunter and vampires. What else lives in this town?" Jason asked in a sarcastic, aggravated way as he went upstairs to check on Ava. As he opened her door, he saw Henry holding her, and they were asleep. He just took a deep breath, left them alone, and went to take a shower to get all the blood off. After he got out of the shower, he decided to sit on the porch. As he walked outside, he saw Sky sitting on the steps. "What are you still doing here? The party has been over for like an hour," Jason asked as he sat down beside her.

"I wanted to say goodnight, but your grandma said you were in the shower, so I decided to wait," Sky said. "We never got to do your cake, so I figured we could look for a shooting star for you to wish on," Sky continued with a smile.

"I have an idea. Follow me." Jason said. He stood up and held out his hand. Sky grabbed his hand and gladly followed. They walked out to Jason's truck, and he put the tailgate down. "It's darker out here. We can actually see the whole sky," Jason said.

Sky backed up to the tailgate but was too short to get up on the tailgate. "Well, I'm short, so I hope you have a plan for how I'm getting up here," Sky said as she laughed.

Jason walked up to her, grabbed her hands and put them around his neck and then put his hands on her waist and picked her up and set her on the tailgate. As he let her go and tried to step back she wouldn't let go and kissed him. Jason was surprised, but he didn't fight her. When she let him go, he stepped back. "I'm not sure what to say to that," Jason blushed.

"Don't say anything," Sky said. Jason could tell she wanted to kiss him again, so he stepped forward and kissed her again, but this time, he put his hand on her face and it turned out very romantic. Sky finally pushed him back and turned her head away. "Stop... I'm sorry... I have to go," Sky said as she jumped down and started to walk away.

Jason grabbed her arm gently. "I'm sorry. Did you not want me to kiss you again?" Jason asked.

"No, you were great, but trust me, you don't want me here right now. We have to take things slow, Jason. I can't tell you why, but please trust that I like you, and tonight was so perfect. I will see you tomorrow," Sky said and started to walk away, then stopped and turned around to ask, "What was wrong with that girl, by the way?"

"Something bit her on the neck. We called an ambulance and her mom," Jason answered. Sky nodded and turned back on her way. While going toward his house, Jason thought about what had happened and smiled as he thought about the kiss. He has been in love with Sky for years and now she kissed him. He didn't care about any other wish. He had already got his wish for years.

When he got back to the porch, he heard a scream and ran inside. As he ran through the door, he heard it again upstairs. Evelyn and Michael came running out of the kitchen, and all three of them ran upstairs. As they entered Ava's room someone was jumping out the window. "Who was that Ava?" Evelyn asked.

"I don't know, but they tried to grab me from my bed. I guess they didn't see Henry," Ava said as she turned and looked at Henry. "He fought for me," Ava said with a relieving smile.

Evelyn looked at Henry with a concerned look and asked. "Are you ok, Henry?"

"I think so," Henry said while taking off his jacket.

"Oh my God, Henry, you're bleeding!" Ava yelled. They all looked at Henry's side, and it looked like some kind of cut.

"Ava, take him to the bathroom and clean him up. We need to go check outside. Henry, stay with Ava," Michael said. Ava ran into the bathroom and grabbed everything out of the cabinet in a panic to clean the cut on Henry.

"Henry, are you coming in here?" Ava asked.

"Yeah, sorry. I guess I'm still trying to figure out what happened," Henry said as he walked into the bathroom.

"Take your shirt off," Ava said.

"Wait… What?" Henry asked confusedly.

"So I can get to the cut," Ava said.

"Oh right, sorry," Henry said as he unbuttoned his shirt. He was trying to avoid eye contact with her. Ava started cleaning the blood off, and Henry just leaned against the wall, staring into space.

"Are you ok, Henry? I can't believe you did that for me. You could have been killed," Ava said.

"Better me than you," Henry said as he brushed Ava's hair from her eye so she could see the cut better. Ava looked up at him with a surprised and mysterious look.

"What…. Ava, what is it?" Henry asked in a scared voice.

"I can't find the cut. I cleaned all the blood off, and it's just not there," Ava answered, trying to locate the scar or cut.

"Well, maybe it's not my blood. I told your grandma I felt fine. I wasn't hurt at all," Henry said. Ava just looked at the floor with a worried look. Henry put his hand on her face, trying to comfort her. As he did, she stepped back against the wall, and he stepped forward. "Ava, I'm fine… Please don't worry… Look at me, Ava," Henry said. As Ava looked up, Henry leaned in and placed his lips on hers. There was a brief pause after the separation of lips that just felt ecstasy against each other.

"I love you, Ava. I said I would protect you, and I did, and I'm fine," Henry broke the silence.

Ava smiled and hugged Henry. "I love you too, Henry," Ava paused, and then Henry continued with a smile while caressing her head against his shoulder. "By the way, where did you get that dress? I know you picked that dress to get my attention."

Ava leaned her head back to see Henry's face. "Well, I guess it worked," Ava said with a big smile.

"You always have my attention, Ava," Henry said as he patted her cheeks lovingly.

CHAPTER 5

The sun was starting to rise, and everyone had been up all night. The house was a mess, and Ava and Henry had been sitting on the couch down stairs all night, waiting for everyone to come home. Henry leaned in to kiss Ava again, and at that very moment, the door flew open, and Jason walked in. "We can't find who did this. We have looked everywhere. I can't believe he got away," Jason said. Ava wanted to tell Jason about her and Henry but figured now was the wrong time. She didn't want him to kill Henry. Jason turned and looked at Ava and Henry sitting on the couch together. Henry got a little scared and got up.

"How deep is your cut? Are you ok?" Jason asked.

"Well about that…. I was cleaning it, and after I had got all the blood off, I couldn't find a cut," Ava said as she stood up from the couch. Henry took his shirt off as Evelyn and Michael came in.

"Healed up good, I see," Michael said.

"Healed up? No one heals that fast… Must have been the other person's blood," Henry said.

"Yeah, that must be what it was," Michael said sarcastically as he walked to the kitchen.

Evelyn gave Michael a look and quickly changed the subject. "I think it's best we have Henry stay again, possibly the whole week, since school is out for a few months for summer. Is that ok with you, Henry?" Evelyn asked.

"It should be fine with my mom. I would really like to stay," Henry said. They all knew that Ava wasn't safe if whoever that was came after her again and that they must have known she didn't have powers to protect herself. Henry walked into the kitchen to call his mom, and Jason stayed with Ava.

"I want you to tell me step by step what exactly happened, Ava," Jason said.

"We were asleep, and I felt someone pulling on me, so I woke up and saw this person standing over me. I screamed, and it woke up Henry, and then it was all kind of a blur. I know Henry jumped up and swung at the person, but not sure if he made contact. It was as if the person flew backward," Ava said.

"You mean like flew backward, as in Henry hit them, and they flew backward?" Jason asked.

"No, I mean, actually flew," Ava replied. Jason looked at his dad and he could tell Michael had something on his mind. No one wanted to really talk about what happened after that. It was very quiet as they waited for Henry to come back into the room. Henry walked in and saw everyone sitting quietly, which made him worry. "So my mom said I could stay. Is everything ok in here?" Henry asked.

"Yes, Jason was just asking exactly what happened," Ava answered.

"Whoever that was went for Ava and I'm not ok with that," Henry said. Jason looked at Henry as he stood up.

"Can we talk in the kitchen, Dad?" Jason asked as he walked by Michael. They walked into the kitchen, and Jason sat down at the table. "Can vampires fly?" Jason asked.

"I'm not sure, Jason, but I think we should lock the house down until we figure everything out. It's the only way to keep everyone safe." Michael said.

Back in the living room, Evelyn and Henry were still trying to comfort Ava. Henry walked over to Ava and sat down beside her to hold her hand and Evelyn looked at them and smiled. "Does Jason know about you two?" Evelyn asked.

"I think so, grandma," Ava said. Evelyn was just trying to talk to Ava about anything to get her mind off of everything.

"I'm going to go to the kitchen to talk to your father," Evelyn said. Evelyn went and sat down at the table to join the conversation. They all had a lot to figure out with all the things going on.

"Let's talk about everything that has happened. We have the hunter, we have the piece needed to free Emma, and we have a vampire running loose. What do we do now, and could all these things be connected?" Jason asked.

Jason looked at Evelyn, who seemed to be lost in thought. "What is it, Grandma?" Jason asked.

"I was just thinking, could it be that the hunter wasn't trying to hurt me? Maybe he is after the vampire. We haven't done anything wrong for the hunter to come after us," Evelyn said.

"What happened the day the hunter came? We never really talked about it. Everyone was caught up with me throwing him through the window," Jason said.

"Well, someone knocked at the door, and when I opened it, I got a bad feeling like something was wrong, so I tried to shut the door back real fast, but he caught it with his hand and pushed it open. I ran into the living room and then into the kitchen and then out the door way by the stairs with him right behind me, which is when you came in and threw him," Evelyn answered.

"Did he have a knife or anything in his hands?" Jason asked.

Evelyn looked at her hands and played back the whole incident in her head, "I don't think so."

"We need to talk to him. We need to know the reason he is here," Jason said.

"How are we going to do that? If he is here to kill us, he will just attack." Michael shared his thoughts.

"I will send a note to him. I will put in the note that I have questions and have no intentions of fighting. I'm also going alone. I don't want anyone to try and fight me on this because I know what I'm doing, and I'm also stronger than everyone else here," Jason said as he got up from the table to get a pen and some paper. Evelyn and Michael agreed to let Jason go alone even though they didn't want to.

Note:

"I need to meet with you alone. I do not want to fight. I have questions that I think you can answer. I will be at the old Oak tree in the park at 11:00 pm tonight.

- Jason."

After writing the note Jason used his powers to send it into the pocket of the hunter. "Now we wait," Jason said. Jason stood up from the table and went back into the living room with Ava and Henry. Jason sat down to tell them of the plan. Evelyn and Michael were still in the kitchen, trying to think of a way to make sure Jason would be alright later.

"We should attach his life to mine. If anything happens to him, it will happen to me as well, and we will know." Michael came up with an idea.

"Jason would never let me do that," Evelyn said.

"Then we don't tell him," Michael said.

"No... he will be very upset if he finds out. I can't do that to him," Evelyn said as she got up to go back to the living room. At that moment, the doorbell rang, and Jason slowly walked to the door to answer it. He stood with his back against the wall with his hand on the door handle.

"Who is it?" Jason asked. "It's Sky... something is hanging on your door," Sky said.

Jason opened the door, and there was a note; it read, *"I will be there."*

"Who is that from?" Sky asked. Jason couldn't answer that so changing the subject was the better idea.

"What are you doing here, Sky? At this time?" Jason asked. Sky looked really upset. Jason didn't know what to do, but he didn't want to turn her away.

"I just needed someone to talk to. My brother and I got into a fight," Sky said.

"Wait right here. I will be right back," Jason said. He ran into the living room and gave the note to Evelyn and told her about Sky then headed back to Sky. "Do you want to take a walk?" Jason asked. Sky smiled and turned around to walk down the steps, so Jason followed her.

They walked for a long time before Sky even looked up from the ground. "I didn't have anywhere else to go. My parents are out of town, and it's just my brother and I at home. I can't be around him right now." Sky said.

"Are you planning to stay out all night?" Jason asked.

"If I can find somewhere to stay, if I go back, we will end up fighting again," Sky said.

"What were you fighting about?" Jason asked.

Sky looked up and then looked at Jason. "It's nothing. I should go."

Sky said. "No, you don't get to do that again. You don't have to answer my question, but you don't get to keep running off," Jason said. Sky just smiled and then walked up to Jason, put her arms around his neck, and then put her head on his shoulder.

"You could stay at my house. My grandma won't mind," Jason offered. Sky raised her head and looked at Jason and kissed him. As she pulled away, Jason smiled, "So I'm guessing that's a yes?" Jason said as he smiled. Sky started laughing and pushed Jason in a flirting way. The two then headed back to the house.

Henry and Ava were still on the couch. Ava had fallen asleep on Henry's shoulder, and Henry had his head lying on top of Ava's. Jason and Sky walked in and saw them. Sky could tell it bothered Jason a little. "Why are you upset?" Sky asked.

"It's my little sister...I just don't know what to think." Jason answered.

"Henry is 16, and your sister is about to be 15. They are just a little over a year apart. I think it's sweet," Sky added as she smiled at Jason. Jason couldn't help but smile back. They then walked into the kitchen where Evelyn and Michael were so they could talk to them.

"Grandma, you remember Sky, right?" Jason asked.

"Yes, I remember her. How are you, sweetie?" Evelyn asked.

"She needs somewhere to stay tonight, her parents are out of town, and her brother and her are fighting. She doesn't want to go back home where he is," Jason answered instead of Sky.

Evelyn hugged Sky, "I'm sorry, sweetie. Of course, you can stay. Remember my rules; the door stays open." Sky smiled and grabbed Jason's hand, and they went up to his room.

"So this is your room, not exactly what I was expecting," Sky said as they walked in.

"What do you mean?" Jason asked.

"It's so clean. Most guys are a mess," Sky answered.

"I'm not most guys," Jason said.

Sky turned and looked at him, "I have noticed."

"Well, let's give you a tour of the rest of the house," Jason said. He took her to his grandma's room and then into the game room, which had doors connected to the bathroom, which then connected to Ava's room and his own, where he kept his door closed. As they walked into the game room, Sky backed out the door and said, "We should just go back to your room."

"Why? Are you ok, Sky?" Jason asked worriedly.

"I just can't go in there, and I can't tell you why," Sky responded.

"Ok, at least you didn't run off," Jason said with a little laugh. Sky just smiled as they started walking back to Jason's room. Ava and Henry were walking into her room as Sky and Jason passed and Sky stopped and ran into Ava's room.

"What happened in here?" Sky asked.

"Well, we don't know. Someone was in my room earlier, but I didn't see who." Ava said.

Sky ran to the bathroom and then directly into Jason's room. As Jason got into his room, Sky was standing turned away from him, "I really wanted to stay, but I need to leave."

"Why can't you stay? I thought you needed to stay away from your brother?" Jason was confused.

"It's very complicated, Jason, but trust me, you do not want me here right now," Sky said as she turned to the door and ran out and down the stairs. Jason tried to catch her to find out what was wrong, but by the time he made it to the front door, Sky was gone.

"What happened, Jason?" Evelyn was curious.

"I'm not sure. She was acting as if something was really bothering her about Ava's room," Jason shrugged.

"Do you think she knows who did it?" Michael asked. Jason just looked confused. And it was almost time to meet the hunter, so he needed to get his mind straight.

"How about we have some cake before you leave?" Evelyn said as she got up to grab some plates. Ava and Henry were headed back to the kitchen while Evelyn was grabbing the cake.

"Hey, we will take some of that," Ava said. They all sat down and ate cake and had some laughs as it got closer to the time Jason had to leave.

Ava started looking at the clock and began to look very sad. "What's wrong, Ava?" Jason questioned.

"What if he kills you?" Ava asked.

"He won't. I will disappear before that happens. I will travel back here if I feel he wants to hurt me. I promise, Ava." Jason reassured her. Ava jumped up and hugged Jason. He was her only brother, and she was very scared he would get hurt. "It's time for me to go, but I will be back, and everything will be fine," Jason said. Everyone took turns hugging him before he left, just in case the worst happened. "Can I talk to you for a minute, Henry?" Jason asked as he walked into the living room, followed by Henry. "I need you to take care of my family. Keep your phone on, call me if anything happens, and keep my sister close. Remember, someone wants her, and they are not getting her." Jason said.

"You got that right," Henry nodded.

As they went back into the kitchen, Michael walked up to him. "I'm proud of you, son. Hurry back, and don't leave us worried for long," he said with a smile. Jason stepped back and disappeared.

As Jason appeared at the park he didn't see anyone. He walked up to the tree and sat down. He figured he would look less threatening sitting against a tree. He was sitting there thinking as a car pulled up. It was the hunter, and he slowly got out and started walking to Jason. As he got close, Jason saw something in his hand.

"Stop! What is that?" Jason said.

"It's my crossbow, and I plan on keeping it," The hunter said. Jason stood up, and the hunter drew his bow.

"This is ridiculous; how are we going to talk when we don't trust each other?" Jason said.

They both stood for a minute, looking at each other. "How about this?" Jason said as he turned around and faced the tree, "I'm trusting you won't shoot me in the back, but trust has to start somewhere."

After a minute, Jason felt something land beside him. As he looked down, it was the crossbow. "You know my name, so it's only fair I know yours," Jason continued. "Can I turn around now? It would be easier to talk."

"Yeah. Just know I'm trusting you as well right now," The hunter said. Jason turned around really slowly.

"My name is Branson." He started as Jason turned around.

"I need to ask a question before we can fully trust each other," Jason said.

"What's that?" Branson asked.

"Are you the hunter that took my mom, Emma?" Jason asked.

"I'm afraid not," Branson answered.

"Then let's move on. We had someone visit our house tonight, and they were not invited. They almost took my sister and got into a fight with my best friend. Do you know anything about that?" Jason asked.

"I might. I have been tracking some vamps for over six months. They just moved here from Arkansas. Every time they move somewhere new, a lot of people die." Branson said. After a moment of silence and looking at each other, not sure what to say, Branson finally said something. "What's your plan?"

"Well, I need to find them, and I could really use your help. Believe me, Branson. My family and I don't want to hurt anyone. We have a home nearby that's been in the family for a while. We just want to live in peace." Jason said.

"So you're saying you want to work together. I don't think that's ever been done before – a warlock and a hunter working on a case together." Branson said while laughing. "Actually, that's exactly what I'm saying, and we could plan everything back at my place," Jason said. Branson stood there for a second, looking at Jason. It was as if he was worried he couldn't trust him. Jason held his hand out to shake his hand and noticed someone running up behind Branson as he grabbed Jason's hand. Jason pulled Branson to him, pushed him down to the ground, and threw the person running up. At that moment, three more people ran out of the woods. Jason then helped Branson up. "Who are these people?" Jason asked.

"I don't know. Where is my bow?" Branson asked as he bent down and grabbed it.

"You can't shoot them all. There are four of them coming in different directions." Jason said.

"Then we run," Branson said.

"Hold on to me!" Jason yelled. Branson grabbed Jason's shoulder with a confused look, and then Jason traveled them to Branson's car. They took off as fast as they could to get away.

"Where are we going now?" Branson asked. Jason just sits quietly for a minute. He was wondering who they were and why they were there. He needed to tell his family. "Let's go to my farm. I need to talk to my family." Jason said.

"I don't think so. A house full of Witches and…."

Jason cut Branson off before he could finish what he was saying. "Do you want to find out what's going on or not?"

"Fine but you're going in first to let them know and to make sure no one is going to try to hurt me. I'm not walking into my grave," Branson said.

"Fine, but you should know. I'm the strongest one in my house, and I was the one that threw you through the window." Jason said. Branson turned to look at Jason for a second, then turned his focus back to the road.

As they pulled up to the farm, Branson looked lost in thought. "Walk with me to the porch, and bringing your weapons wouldn't be a bad idea since whoever the people at the park are might follow us to the farm. Just don't have them drawn when we walk in, and you will be fine. We need everyone to know that we are friends. Well, at least friendly," Jason said as they got out of the car.

He turned to walk to the house, and Branson stopped him. "I just wanted to thank you for saving me back there. I had my guard down, and I know if it wasn't for you, I might not be here."

"Just remember that and return the favor if you can one day," Jason said. They walked into the house, and Jason kept Branson behind him to shield him from anything in case they didn't give them a chance to explain everything. They walked into the living room, and everyone was sitting and talking. They saw Branson but just sat there looking at them both as if they were waiting for Jason to explain. "First off, this isn't the hunter that took Mom. The second thing we ran into some trouble at the park - Not with each other. We were attacked." Jason started. Ava jumped up and ran to Jason, crying. "I'm so glad you're back. I was so scared."

"So, are you going to tell us why he is here?" Michael questioned. Branson stepped out from behind Jason and held his hand out offering a handshake to Michael. Michael stood up and shook his hand.

"Your son saved my life. I will not hurt anyone in this room; that's a promise." Branson said.

Evelyn saw a cut on Branson's arm and said, "You're hurt."

Branson lifted his arm to look at it and continued, "Must have happened when Jason threw me to the ground."

"To save your life," Jason interrupted in a get-over-it voice.

"It still hurt," Branson said. Jason just rolled his eyes.

"Let's get you cleaned up. Follow me," Evelyn said.

Branson followed Evelyn to the kitchen, where she had a first aid kit ready for Jason in case the meeting ended badly. As she was bandaging his arm, Branson kept looking at her and then said, "You know, the day I showed up, I was honestly trying to talk to you. I didn't want to hurt you. I could tell you were sweet and wasn't a bad witch."

Evelyn looked up at him and asked, "Then why did you chase me?"

"I shouldn't have, but I just wanted to talk. I figured if I caught you, I could explain, but then Buffy the hunter-slayer showed up and threw me through a window before I could get a word out." Branson answered. Evelyn started laughing so hard that everyone came into the kitchen to find out what was going on.

"Grandma, are you ok?" Ava asked.

"Yes. Oh goodness, yes," Evelyn answered while wiping tears from her eyes from laughing so hard.

"So this is your family," Branson said.

"Yes! Sorry, this is Ava, my sister, Evelyn, my grandma, Michael, my dad, and..." Branson cut Jason off. "This is Henry the..." Branson looked behind Jason, where he saw Evelyn shaking her head no. and knew what she was talking about and changed what he was going to say. "The boy down the road." Branson resumed.

"He's been my best friend for years," Jason said.

"So what do we do if the people follow you here?" Michael asked.

"We fight," Branson said as he took the large bag off his shoulder and threw it on the table. He opened the bag and started pulling out weapons. He had everything, from small knives to large guns. He had it all. "We use these. Who here has ever fired a gun?" Evelyn and Michael grabbed a gun. "I shot my Grandpa's shotgun once," Henry said.

"Once is good enough. I want you to take this and little witch up to her room. If anything, and I mean anything, comes in there, you shoot. It won't kill them, but it hurts, and they know that," Branson said as he handed Henry a shotgun.

"I don't need anything. You know what I can do," Jason said. "Yeah, I do, and I need you to place a spell on the farm," Branson said.

Jason looked at his grandma and dad and asked. "What spell is he talking about? Like the one mom did?"

"He doesn't know how to do one? Do you have any potions to place one, Evelyn?" Branson asked.

"No, but I can teach Jason to do it with his powers," Evelyn said.

Jason followed her into the living room. "With the spell, you will sense if someone gets close to the farm. If the spell is done right, you will get a vision of them. You need to picture a wall of energy around the farm that alerts you as soon as someone crosses it," Evelyn said.

Jason sat down and tried to focus. "I can't do it. There is just too much on my mind," Jason said in an aggravated voice.

"Yes, you can. You're the only one in this house who can do magic without spells. Just clear your mind and try again," Evelyn said as she smiled, hugged Jason, and walked back to the kitchen. Jason closed his eyes and focused and visualized the wall, and he felt his power burst from his body. He opened his eyes and knew it was done. He got up and walked back to the kitchen.

"So Henry doesn't know what he is?" Branson asked.

"No, and it's not our place to tell him," Evelyn said.

"He could really help us if he knew. You know that, right?" Branson confirmed.

Evelyn just walked away. Michael walked over to the table and started looking at everything laid out on the table. At that moment, Jason walked back into the room. "We need to tell him what happened the other night," Jason said.

"What happened when and where?" Branson said as he turned to Jason.

"A girl got bit at my party, and we think it was a vampire. Do you think it's the vamps you're looking for?" Jason asked.

"Could be, and it could be who attacked us in the park," Branson said.

"Jason. Can we talk to you for a second?" Evelyn asked. Jason joined his grandma and father in the hall.

"So are we just going to work with a hunter now? I mean, he knows who we are, and did you forget the last hunter around put your mom away?" Michael started.

"I don't think we have a choice. He could help us, and we need the help. He might even be able to help us get Mom back. She didn't even do anything wrong, and if we tell him, maybe he will help," Jason said.

"I just don't trust him," Evelyn added.

"I don't either. We don't have to trust him. We don't even have to like him. We just need to work with him. Please trust me on this. We need him, and he needs us," Jason said. Michael and Evelyn looked at each other for a second and then looked back at Jason.

"Alright… I just hope you know what you're doing." Michael said. As they walked back into the kitchen, Evelyn could tell everyone was tired.

"Maybe we should try to get some rest," Evelyn said.

"Alright, grandma. I will see you in the morning," Ava took her leave. Henry just looked at Evelyn and smiled as he followed Ava to her room to protect her as she slept.

"I will take the first watch," Branson said.

"I think I will join you," Michael said in an annoyed voice.

"Can you two just please get along? We need to work together." Jason said. They both looked at Jason and then Michael went to the front porch and Branson to the back porch so they could watch both sides of the house. Evelyn hugged Jason and then went to bed. Jason decided to sleep on the couch since he was the only one who had active powers that he could use without a spell. He would be in the middle if anything happened.

CHAPTER 6

The night seemed to go on forever. Everyone was asleep but Michael and Branson. It was pushing 4:30 am, and they were both getting tired. Michael decided coffee was a good idea. As he headed inside, he thought about Branson on the back porch. He went to the kitchen to make coffee. As he grabbed himself a cup what Jason said just kept playing over in his head.

"Good grief… why can't I just drink coffee," Michael said as he grabbed another cup and headed for the back door.

"I brought you some coffee. I wasn't sure how you liked it, so I just gave you my favorite-black coffee with one sugar," Michael said as he handed the cup to Branson.

"Thanks; I know that it's weird having me here. I honestly just want to help. Your son saved my life, and I owe him. He's a good boy. Supernatural or not, I think of him as a friend. I have actually been sitting here all night thinking about what happened and how fast he could have left me there to die but didn't. I won't let another hunter close to your family," Branson said as he looked out into the dark field.

"Would you be willing to help us with something?" Michael asked.

"If I can… just name it," Branson replied promptly.

"My wife, Jason's mother, was taken by a hunter a long time ago and put in something like her very own prison," Michael said with a long pause.

"May I ask what she did?" Branson asked.

"Nothing! The hunter wanted to be with her, and she chose me, so he imprisoned her out of jealousy," Michael answered.

"Well, the door wouldn't be any of ours because we would have known if he used them, and he would have had to explain himself, which he wouldn't want to do. With that being said, some hunters run rouge like me in a way, but they just hate everything about the supernatural and would have killed your boy and his mother. They have learned to make their own prison doors from the magic they have picked up along the way," Branson said.

"Can you help us get her back?" Michael asked.

"If we make it through this fight alive, I will gladly help your family save her," Branson said as he stood up and held his hand out to shake Michael's hand.

After Michael shook Branson's hand, he had to break the silence. "How about a sandwich?"

"That actually sounds great. I'm honestly starving," Branson said.

As they walked in Jason was standing in the kitchen. "I got hungry, and it woke me up. I see you two are getting along." Jason said.

"Yeah, he isn't so bad," Michael continued in a joking way. "We came in because we are hungry too. What do you think about sandwiches? I can make them."

"Or I could make them," Jason said while shrugging his shoulders, and then, with a wave of his hand three huge amazing sandwiches appeared with all the fixings.

"I could really get used to this. Can I live here?" Branson said while laughing. The guys sit down to eat and to tell Jason about Branson's plan to help save his mom.

"Well, I plan to live, so be ready to keep your word. Let's not tell Ava, though. I just don't want to get her hopes up in case something happens," Jason said.

"You mean, in case I die," Branson said.

"No one is going to die in this house. This family has been through enough," Jason said in a powerful voice.

"So I'm family now?" Branson said while smiling. Jason and Michael just smiled.

While the guys were sitting there talking, they heard something outside. Jason jumped up and wanted to run outside, but he also wanted to run upstairs to check on his sister. Branson saw Jason being torn between the two.

"I've got her, Jason. Go," Branson said as he headed toward the stairs.

"Keep my sister safe at all costs," Jason said as he ran outside. Michael was right behind Jason to see what the noise was. As they got outside, Jason remembered the spell he put up, and he didn't see anything, so if they were there, they had to already be inside the farm as it went up. Michael and Jason didn't see anything. As Branson ran through Ava's door, it woke up Henry, who jumped up and grabbed Branson by the neck and shoved him against the wall. As Branson looked into Henry's eyes, he knew he had to do something, or he was going die. "Henry, it's me, Branson. We heard something outside. I'm here to help in case someone breaks in," Branson said while barely able to breathe. At that moment, Jason ran into the room.

"Henry, drop him!" Jason yelled. As Henry turned to look at Jason he saw the look on Jason's face.

"Oh my God, Henry, your eyes," Jason said. There was a mirror right beside Jason, and when Henry looked, his eyes were a dark yellow and very glossy, which made his eyes almost glow in the light that was coming in from the doorway of the hall. He let go of Branson and ran to the mirror.

"What is that? What's wrong with my eyes?" Henry yelled. As soon as Henry turned to Jason, his eyes were back to normal.

"Look again, Henry. They are normal now. Let's go downstairs and talk to my grandma," Jason said while freaking out. All the yelling woke up Ava, and she saw Henry's eyes as well. She was still trying to figure out what happened during all the drama and what was wrong with Henry. As the boys ran downstairs, she followed in hopes of finding answers herself. As Jason and Henry ran into the kitchen, Evelyn was already there, and she was on the phone with someone.

"I heard everything. You two just sit down. We need to wait on someone," Evelyn said as she grabbed cups to fix drinks. Jason sat down on one side of Henry, and Ava sat on the other and grabbed Henry's hand to try and comfort him.

"That was a very tight grip he had, I'm guessing," Michael said while looking at Branson.

"What do you mean?" Branson asked. Michael pointed at a small mirror in the living room. Branson walked to the living room and saw a scratch across his neck that was bleeding.

"I will get the first aid kit again," Evelyn said.

As Evelyn walked back into the living room, there was a knock at the door. She walked over and opened the door, and Henry's mom walked in. "Hi, Sandy. The boys are in the kitchen," Evelyn said.

The boys heard Evelyn from the kitchen. "What's my mom doing here?" Henry asked. As Sandy walked into the kitchen, she walked up behind Henry and hugged him and then walked around the table and sat down in front of him. "Hello, son! I guess we need to have a talk."

Henry looked at Jason and then at Ava. He was worried and scared of what she was going to say. "I heard what happened, and I need to tell you that you're not crazy, and we will all be here with you through it all. You know Jason's secret and now it's time you know your own. You're a werewolf, Henry. As am I and your father," Sandy said.

Henry looked terrified. "So I'm going to grow hair and fangs and run on all fours. This is insane, Mom," Henry said in fear—anything to make it sound not true to him.

"You watch too many movies, son. Werewolves are not much different than we are now. When you turn, you will have glowing eyes, strength, k9 teeth, and sharp nails that can break the skin," Sandy said before being cut off.

"Yeah, no kidding," Branson said. Henry turned around to see Evelyn cleaning a cut on Branson's neck.

"Oh my God, did I do that? Is he going to turn now?" Henry said while freaking out.

"No, it doesn't work like that. We can't really turn anyone. You are born this way or made by a witch. The same goes for vampires. All witches and warlocks have a werewolf. You protect each other. You guys were meant to be friends from the beginning. When a witch gets close to their powers, a werewolf will come into their life and will turn their first time when their witch or warlock is in trouble," Sandy said.

"So he is my best friend and my protector?" Jason asked.

"Yes, Jason. And you are his," Evelyn answered.

"Jason, I was your mother's protector. I'm so sorry I wasn't there for her when she was taken. I was on my way, but I wasn't fast enough. She needed me, and I wasn't there," Sandy said as she started crying.

"It's not your fault. If you had been there, you might have been taken yourself," Evelyn said as she walked over and hugged Sandy. Ava has been sitting and listening to everyone and only had one thing on her mind. Evelyn saw that Ava was in deep thought and asked, "Are you ok, Ava?" Evelyn asked.

"What happens if a witch and werewolf get married and have kids? Is it even possible? I have just been putting things together. If Jason is a full warlock because mom was half witch and dad was half warlock, then I will be a full witch. What happens if a witch and a werewolf want to be together?" Ava asked as she looked over at Henry with a tear streaming down her cheek.

"I don't think it has ever happened. Most people date mortals. That's why there are more half-witches and warlocks out there than full," Evelyn said. Everyone just sat quietly for a minute to process all the information they had just learned.

"Wait, did you say vampires have babies?" Jason asked.

"Yes. They are much like us," Sandy said and then turned towards Evelyn. "We will leave you kids in here to talk about everything. I need to speak to Evelyn alone."

"So Ava and Henry is an item now? Are we ok with that?" Sandy asked.

"Well! I know she is safe with him. He has already protected her once," Evelyn said.

"What do you mean?" Sandy asked.

"We had someone come in the house, and they ended up in Ava's room. Henry was in there lying down with her to keep her calm after a very stressful night and fought the person off," Evelyn answered.

"Wait, what! I know you will take care of my son, but I need to know these things, Evelyn," Sandy looked disappointed.

"I honestly was going to call you over today to let you know about everything. It's just been one thing after another," Evelyn said as Branson walked into the room.

"I am about to go sit and watch the back to make sure everything is clear. Just wanted to let you know I'm not going anywhere," Branson said.

"And who are you? I have never seen you here before," Sandy asked Branson.

"My name is Branson. I'm a hunter," Branson said as he tried to shake her hand.

Sandy turned to Evelyn. "You let a hunter in your house with the kids? What is wrong with you?" Sandy yelled, which got everyone's attention and they came running into the room.

"It's not like that. He is trying to help us. He is after the vampires. He won't hurt us," Jason answered.

"Jason saved my life, and I am going to return the favor by keeping everyone in this house safe. As a matter of fact, you might want to talk to your son. He almost killed me," Branson said as he turned to Henry.

"Let's just all calm down. I know it's not ideal to have a hunter in the house, and I know there is someone after us that might be a vampire. We honestly need all the help we can get," Jason said.

Sandy stood there for a minute looking at Branson and then slowly walked over to him. "Fine, you can stay, but know this. I have killed three hunters, and one more isn't going to keep me up at night. Don't you dare lay a hand on my son," Sandy warned.

Henry and Jason couldn't believe what they had just heard. They stayed quiet, but they both wanted to ask questions. "There is something else you should know. He is going to help us get Emma back," Michael interrupted.

"Can you do that?" Sandy asked as she looked at Branson.

"I'm going to try my best. From what I have heard, she doesn't deserve what happened to her," Branson paused and then continued, "The sun is coming up. We need to get ready for tonight. They will more than likely come tonight."

"Because vampires only come out at night, right?" Henry asked.

"Again, son, too much TV. It's harder to see at night for us, and they can see very well but they do come out during the day. They just don't hunt during the day. Easier to hide at night, and they are very fast," Sandy said.

"You boys need to go get wood—enough for each window and door. We need to block up every entrance. We have to keep them from getting in because they are very strong," Evelyn said.

"Alright, grandma. If anything happens, call me. We can be back fast," Jason said.

"Take your sister. She needs to stay close to you because you can travel and get her out of harm's way fast," Michael said.

As they started to leave, Jason pulled Branson aside. "Keep my family safe," Jason said. Branson gave Jason a little smile. He knew his family would be fine until he got back.

Ava ran out and got in the front this time, and Henry got in the back seat behind her. Jason drove to the lumber yard and sent Henry in to tell them what they needed, "While Henry is inside, I need to talk to you, Ava… I don't mind that you and Henry are dating… I just want you to be careful. We are not sure if you two can even… well, how do I say this," Jason said before being cut off by Ava. "Oh my God, Jason, I'm only fourteen. I'm not thinking about that right now," Ava said.

"What? No… God, No… but that's a good point. I was talking about just being together in general. How would everything work out? Can you have kids with him, and what would they be like? Will it be dangerous? You will be a witch soon, and we need to know if it's safe. I just don't want you to get hurt," Jason said.

"I know you care about me, Jason, and I love you for that. You're my brother, and I know you will always be there for me, but I also love Henry, and he loves me. I promise we will find out all the facts before we just get married. Besides, that would be many years away. I turn fifteen in 2 days, and I'm not looking to get married anytime soon," Ava said with a little laugh. Jason just smiled and grabbed Ava's hand. He really just wanted to be a good big brother. Henry got back in the truck.

"They said to pull to the back so they can load the truck," Henry said.

"How many were we able to get?" Jason asked as he drove to the back.

"I bought plenty and extra. I wanted to make sure they have to work to get into the house," Henry replied.

"Good. Just to let you two know. If they get in, I'm sending you both to my truck, and Henry, I want you to run with Ava. I don't want to know where you are going. Just keep my sister safe until I find you. So when we get home, I'm giving you my keys, and I want you to hold onto them," Jason said.

"But what about you, Jason? You are my brother; we can't just leave you." Ava interrupted.

"You can and you will! I can fight better knowing you are safe somewhere. I won't have to keep trying to keep them away from you because you won't be there," Jason said.

Ava just sat back, looking out the window. She didn't like the idea, but she couldn't make Jason let her stay. She didn't have powers yet, so she understood, but she still didn't want to leave him or any of the others. There was a knock on the window with a guy waving him out. "We must be loaded down. Back to the house, I guess," Henry said.

Back at the house, the adults were talking. "If they get in, we will send the kids away," Sandy said.

"Jason isn't going to leave. He is going to want to fight," Michael said.

"I know, but we will have to make him leave. He won't be any good to anyone dead," Evelyn said.

"I don't see how we can make Jason do anything. Have you guys not seen what I have?" Branson asked.

"What does he mean?" Sandy asked.

"You know the stories about the kids who have both magical parents are very powerful. Well, it's true," Evelyn said.

"He has more power than I have ever seen," Branson said.

"He doesn't need spells. He can create things from thin air and do so much more." Michael said.

"So it's true, he could control them," Sandy said.

"I don't know if we should chance it. It takes someone with a lot of experience to do that, and Jason is new at this," Evelyn added.

"Yeah, it's just too dangerous," Michael agreed.

"Does he even know how to get into people's heads yet?" Sandy asked.

"We are not sure, but either way, there isn't enough time to teach him," Evelyn answered.

"The children being safe should be a top priority in any case, and if sending them away does that, then we have to. Would you mind helping me bring in some tools to board up the house?" Michael asked as he turned to Branson.

"I don't mind," Branson said as he followed Michael. They went out to the shed and grabbed as many tools as they could carry. Evelyn and Sandy were inside fixing food to keep in a bag in case the kids had to run. As Michael and Branson were headed back to the house, the kids pulled up in the truck.

"Where do you want the wood, Dad?" Jason asked.

"Back the truck up to the barn. We will unload it there and only bring in what we need," Michael said.

Jason backed the truck all the way into the barn and handed Henry the keys. "Don't forget what we talked about. This barn will hide you both as well, but once you're in the truck, don't take too long, just in case," Jason said. Henry didn't say anything, but he couldn't believe Jason wanted them to leave everyone there.

As Jason walked up to the house, he thought about something. "Why didn't I see or sense you when you walked onto the farm? Grandma said that I could see anyone that crossed it." Jason asked Sandy as he walked in the door.

Sandy smiled at Jason and then pulled out a beautiful amulet that was hidden under her clothes. "Your mother made me this for my 18th birthday. It hides me from others being able to see me when I cross spell castings, and it also keeps me hidden from psychics," Sandy said.

"Something else you should know, though, is that the spell only last 24 hours, and since you're still learning, yours probably ended early, so we will need to place another soon," Evelyn said.

Jason was still looking at the amulet in Sandy's hand. He took it from her hands and looked at it for a few minutes in quiet. "My mom made this? I wish I could have had the time to get to know her," Jason said.

"You will! I will help you find your mom," Branson said as he walked in behind him.

Everyone gathered in the living room to talk over a plan. "Alright! The boys will bring in supplies, and the men will hang the wood. Us girls will head to the kitchen to prepare drinks and food for breaks and then we will help move furniture so we can have more room in case they make it inside," Evelyn said.

"Grandma, don't forget I can bring wood in without going outside," Jason said.

"I know, sweetie and we might need that skill later, but for now, let's do it the old-fashioned way. We don't need you to tire yourself out." Evelyn said. Jason and Henry went to the barn to grab wood, and the guys started getting things ready by taking down the curtains. As Jason and Henry were headed back to the house, Sky pulled up.

"Jason, look! Sky is here. What are we going to do?" Henry asked.

"I will get rid of her. Do you have this?" Jason asked as he stepped back.

"Yeah! Just get her out of here so she doesn't get hurt," Henry said. Jason walked over to Sky's car as she was getting out. "Hey… what are you doing here, Sky?" Jason asked.

"Just thought I would visit. I missed you," Sky said as she saw Henry and the guys hanging wood on the window.

Jason noticed her looking out the window and stepped in front of her to try and distract her. "Well, I have missed you too. I'm glad you stopped by, but," Jason said, but Sky cut him off. "What are they doing? Is everything ok, Jason?" She asked.

"Honestly, you know what? We will be fine. Just… well… I can't really explain, but we will be fine. I do really need to go help though. Can I call you tomorrow?" Jason asked as he kissed Sky goodbye.

"Sure, but just know you can tell me anything, Jason. I can help… I can't tell you how… just know I can help," Sky said as she got back in her car. They waved bye and Jason went back to work on the house.

As Jason walked onto the porch, he couldn't stop thinking about what Sky said. She must really like him to want to help and not even know what's wrong. "What did Sky want?" Henry asked.

"She just wanted to see me," Jason said with a smile.

"Looks like she loves you too, bro," Henry teased Jason.

"I don't know about all that, but she definitely likes me," Jason said.

"Are you boys going to help or sit around and talk about girls?" Michael asked.

"Alright, Dad, we hear you," Jason said, and then the boys let out a muffled laugh. The girls were still in the kitchen fixing food and drinks for everyone because they knew it was going to be a long day and night. The guys had finally boarded up the whole first floor, but the second floor still needed to be done. "We can do it, Dad. You and Branson need to rest. You have both been up all night." Jason said. As the boys headed up the stairs, Jason stopped.

"What's wrong?" Henry asked.

"I can't stop thinking about what Sky said earlier," Jason answered.

"Well, what did she say?" Henry asked.

"She said she could help me… but she wouldn't tell me how," Jason said.

"You know girls… they are always trying to help," Henry said.

"This was different. It was like she already knew or something," Jason said as he started walking up the stairs again.

"You mean like maybe she is a witch?" Henry questioned. Jason stopped and turned around to look at Henry. "I'm just saying, with everything we have seen, would it really be that farfetched?" Henry continued. Jason turned back around, and they continued to Ava's room first. They both wanted to make sure she was very safe.

The house was finally done, and everyone was headed to the living room except Michael and Branson, who were already sleeping in the living room. If these are vampires that have entirely embraced what they are, then they will be very dangerous. "I need you to all stay close to Jason so he can protect everyone," Evelyn said to the kids.

"Wait so there are vampires that are nice?" Jason asked.

"Actually, yes! We are werewolves, and we are nice, but some think people are food and stay in their pack," Sandy answered.

"Their pack… what do you mean?" Asked Henry asked.

"We are part of a pack, just like Jason is part of a coven," Sandy said.

"The movies were correct on one thing. The only way to kill a vampire is by a wooden stake to the heart, cutting off the head, or by magic," Evelyn added.

"Magic? How do I kill them with magic?"

"You can crush their heart with magic," Evelyn said.

Jason looked at Henry with a worried look. "Guess my magic can be used for bad to then. If I can do that to a vampire, I can just imagine what I could do to a mortal," Jason said.

"Yes and that's why you can never let your magic control you because if you turn bad, Henry does too," Sandy said.

"You two are linked, and it only takes one of you to lose yourself for it to spread between you both," Evelyn said, and it paused the conversation, at least for then.

Jason, Ava, and Henry went into the kitchen to eat. "We need to stay close to each other. I will go with you if things get bad. Grandma is right. I need to stay close to you both," Jason said. Henry took Jason's keys out of his pocket and handed them to him.

"I wonder if we have ice cream. That sounds like some great comfort food right now," Ava said as she stood up.

"When are you going to learn Ava?" Jason said with a smile.

"Grandma said to save your strength," Ava said.

"It's fine… I will be fine… just sit and tell me what kind." Jason said. While the kids were in the kitchen, Evelyn woke up Michael and Branson, and the adults were in the living room planning for that night.

"We need to put the kids together in Ava's room and keep Ava hidden," Michael said.

"Just leave her with Henry. He will keep her safe. Trust me, I have seen it firsthand," Branson said.

"Then you and I will post up outside like we did last night," Michael said while looking at Branson.

"Jason and I can fight inside. But if a bunch come running up, we need you guys inside, so don't stand out there trying to take them all on alone," Evelyn said.

"We will run in if the number is bigger than two to one. We will play it safe," Michael continued, "I'm going to talk to the pack and tell them what is going on. It might take a couple days, but they could help kill off the vampires."

"That's a good idea. I'm going to check on the kids, and I will let them know," Evelyn said. As she walked into the kitchen, she saw Ava sitting there with a burger and fries.

"Where did this come from?" Evelyn asked. Ava and Henry just looked at each other but stayed quiet.

"Jason, you didn't… did you listen to anything I said?" Evelyn asked.

"You haven't seen how strong I am, Grandma. I have done way more in one day than conjure a burger," Jason said.

"I know Jason, but you can still make yourself weak if you're not careful, and we need your full power tonight. It's going to take everything you have later to take on all the vampires and keep your sister safe," Evelyn said. Jason just looked at the table and started thinking about later. Just how many vampires were out there, and how could he fight them? So many things were going through his mind.

CHAPTER 7

The day seemed to go on forever, and everyone had their plan down. They knew what to do and when, but Jason still felt as if Ava and Henry shouldn't be there.

"Jason, it's time to do the spell," Evelyn said. Jason walked into the living room and sat down, and Evelyn stayed close to him with the magic book in case he couldn't do it. At that moment, someone started knocking at the door. She handed the book to Jason and walked to the door. Jason opened the book to take a look and the third page he turned to was a spell for the necklace Sandy had. He didn't know how to conjure the enchanted necklace, but he could read the spell, and all he needed was an ordinary necklace that he could conjure. He closed his hands and pictured a necklace and opened his hands and he had it. Now he just needed to enchant it and then he could give it to Sky. After enchanting the necklace, Evelyn walked back in.

"Jason, you have a visitor," Evelyn said. He got up and walked to the door and saw Sky holding a basket.

"I know you said you were busy earlier, so I thought I would make some cookies to comfort you," Sky said.

"Thank you! Do you want to walk out on the porch for a minute?" Jason asked as he walked outside. Sky followed him, and Jason took the basket, set it on the railing of the porch, and took out a cookie.

"These are amazing. You're a really good cook, Sky," Jason praised.

"I know," Sky said with a big smile.

"So the house is fully boarded up, and you're sure you can't tell me why?" Sky said as she turned to Jason.

"I really can't, but I can tell you everything will be fine," Jason said as Sky started to walk away.

"Alright! Well, I will see you tomorrow. I hope you enjoy those cookies," Sky said while smiling.

"Wait… Sky… I need to tell you something. I have to say this before I lose the nerve to. I love you. I have loved you for years. I know we didn't really know each other before but I knew I wanted to be with you since I first met you," Jason said as he walked over to Sky.

"I love you too, Jason," Sky said as she leaned in and kissed Jason.

"I have something for you. I want you to wear it every day so you will remember me every time you look in the mirror," Jason said as he held out the necklace. Sky smiled so big and turned around for Jason to put it on her. She loved it but felt as if Jason was saying goodbye.

"You will be here tomorrow, right?" Sky asked.

"I plan to be," Jason said as he kissed her forehead while giving her a big hug. He let her go and told her bye, then grabbed the basket and went back inside.

"Is she gone?" Evelyn asked.

"Yeah, she is gone. I just wish I could tell her everything," Jason sighed.

"I know you do, but their response isn't always what you expect," Evelyn said.

"Time to do the spell," Michael said. Jason sat back down with Evelyn close by while Henry and Ava were in the kitchen.

"Do you think any of us are going to die tonight?" Ava asked.

"I don't want to lie to you, Ava. I don't know. I just know I want you to stay very close to me. They will have to kill me before they will get to you," Henry said as he grabbed Ava and hugged her.

"Alright, it's up," Jason said.

"Let's take turns napping until fully dark. Three at a time for thirty minutes," Evelyn said. Ava, Henry, and Jason went first. Ava and Henry were in her room watching a movie and fell asleep. Jason was in his room but couldn't fall asleep. He was too worried and couldn't stop thinking about Sky.

It had been twenty-five minutes, and Jason was still awake, so he decided just to go back downstairs and tell someone else to take a nap. As soon as he got downstairs, he started getting lightheaded and then saw seven people run through the pasture and then there was a crash outside. Jason ran into the living room. Michael and Branson were still inside, so no one knew what it was. "I'm going out alone," Jason said as he ran to the door.

"No, you're not! What if they are out there?" Michael said.

"I'm the only one with an active power. I can take care of myself," Jason said as he opened the door and walked out. There was a rock on the porch that someone had thrown at the porch, and it hit the metal trash can, almost like they just wanted to get their attention. When Jason turned around to go back inside, there was a knife in the door holding a letter. The note said: "Send out Branson, or we take the house."

Jason took the note inside to show everyone. "So they want me?" Branson asked.

"Yeah, but that's not going to happen. You're not like the other hunters. You don't deserve this," Jason said.

"That's not your decision. If it will save everyone here, I'm going out there," Branson said as he walked toward the door.

"Wait… just wait a second. How do we know they are telling the truth? What if you go out there, and they kill you and then come after us? That is just one less person fighting for us. We need you alive. We protect the family," Jason said. Branson just looked around at everyone.

"What he said," Michael said.

"We fight together and die together," Ava added.

Jason turned to see Henry and Ava standing in the stairwell. "Agreed," Jason said as he threw them both a stake. Jason opened the door and threw the note outside so they would see that it was no deal. At that moment, Henry took Ava back to her room and shut and locked the door. Ava grabbed Henry's hand tightly and stood beside him, yet behind his arm for protection. Jason was waiting in the middle of the living room. Everyone was ready to stand their ground the best they could when there was a thunderous knock at the door. "We are prepared to fight. When you're ready you come on in. My mother wasn't scared of you, and neither am I!" Jason yelled.

"Are they coming in?" Ava asked Henry.

"I only hear Jason right now. I don't think they are inside," Henry responded.

At that moment, there was a loud crash in the kitchen. Henry ran to the bedroom door and looked down the stairs to make sure no one was coming upstairs, and when he turned to talk to Ava, she was gone.

"Was that the window in the kitchen?" Michael asked.

"Grandma and Sandy are in there!" Jason yelled as he ran to the kitchen. There was a big mess as soon as they walked in. "Where are they?" Michael asked.

Branson strolled through the mess. "Looks like they ran out the back," Branson said. The guys ran out the back door as fast as they could and saw Sandy standing there holding a Vampire, and Evelyn was gone.

"Where is she? Tell me now," Sandy said. As they got closer, they could see Sandy's eyes, and they were the color Henry's were when he wolfed out. She was holding the Vampire from behind with her nails around the throat.

"Where is my grandma?" Jason yelled.

"I don't know, and he isn't talking. We were standing in the kitchen, and the window broke and this one and one other came through the window. The other vampire grabbed Evelyn and ran out, and I was shoved against the wall. I chased this one outside and caught him before he could run away. What do you want me to do with him?" Sandy asked as she looked at Jason and wrapped the vampire up into a tighter headlock so he couldn't get loose.

"Bring him inside. Don't let him escape," Jason said. As they all walked inside Jason was trying to think of a plan when Henry ran into the room.

"They have Ava!" Henry yelled.

"What? How?" Jason yelled.

"She was standing there, and I turned away for one second, and she was gone. Jason, we have to save her," Henry was panicking.

"They have grandma, too," Jason said as he turned to look at the vampire.

"Jason, travel them back here," Henry said.

"He can't. We have chains that repel against traveling and keep the person from using magic, and she is covered in them," the vampire said after being tired of escaping Sandy's grip.

"Then we go get them," Jason said.

"I'm in," Henry said.

"How are we going to keep him here? If we sit him down, won't he get away?" Jason asked.

"You can use your magic," Branson said.

"My magic? I don't know what you mean." Jason asked.

"We can enchant a rope and tie him to a chair with it. He won't be able to break it," Michael said.

"I think we have rope in the attic," Jason said. Henry ran to the attic to look for a rope and found that the window in the attic wasn't covered. After finding the rope, he ran back downstairs to Jason.

"I know how the one that got Ava got in. The window in the attic wasn't covered," Henry said as he looked at Jason.

"We forgot that window. He didn't have to make a sound. We let him right in," Jason sighed.

"Don't beat yourself up, Jason. We will get them back," Michael said.

"Let's tie him up," Branson said. "This will have to be enchanted so he doesn't break loose," Branson said as he tied him up. Jason then enchanted the rope.

"Henry and I are going alone. Stay here in case they come back. We will get them back," Jason said.

"You two, be careful and stick together. Don't let them separate you. You're both stronger together," Sandy said as she took both their hands. Jason and Henry hugged Sandy and then ran out the door toward Jason's truck. They jumped in the truck and headed up the driveway.

"Where are we even going, Jason?" Henry questioned.

"I saw where they ran through the pasture. It was down by the creek. That's where we should start," Jason replied. As they pulled up to the creek, Jason sat there for a minute. "When we find them, I'm traveling them back to the house, and you and I are going to kill them all. My mom let them live, and this is the outcome. I won't make that mistake," Jason added. The boys opened their doors, and before Jason's foot hit the ground, a vampire ran up, grabbed him, and shoved him back inside the truck. He couldn't get his hands up to throw him, and the vampire was choking him. Jason was starting to worry that he would die as it was all happening so fast, and then something or someone ripped the vampire off of him, and Jason fell out of the truck and onto the ground on his hands and knees. "Jason, are you ok?" Henry said as he ran to Jason.

"Yeah, thanks, man… he had me for sure. The steering wheel had my right arm blocked, and my left arm got wrapped in the seatbelt. Thank you for saving me," Jason said.

"Yeah…about that… it wasn't me," Henry said. Jason slowly looked up at Henry.

"Then who was it?" Jason asked.

As the boys looked out into the trees, a person was standing there, and they couldn't see who it was because it was too dark. The person started running toward them, which scared them, but then it ran to the front of the truck and grabbed another vampire, took a bite from its neck, and then threw them to the ground and staked them in the heart. The person slowly turned, and they couldn't believe who it was. "SKY!" Jason yelled. "What are you doing here, and how did you do that?"

Sky could see Jason was a little scared of her and worried. "It's fine. I won't hurt you or Henry," Sky said.

"You're covered in blood, Sky. Did you stop the other one, too?" Henry asked. "I understand now… everything makes sense… you're a vampire," Jason said.

"Yes, I am… my family is different, and we don't kill people. We live off of bagged human blood. We own a blood drive company and sell to other vampires like us," Sky said as she bent down to help Jason up. She held out her hand and waited to see if Jason would take her hand, which would mean he trusted her. Jason smiled as he looked at her and took her hand.

"So you know what I am?" Jason asked.

"I do, and so does my family. We know what you are too, Henry," Sky said.

"That's why your brother hates me," Jason guessed.

"He doesn't hate you, but he knows you can kill us… he is just scared for me," Sky said.

"Guys, I hate to break this up, but we still have a problem," Henry said.

"What is it?" Sky asked.

"The vampires took my sister and my grandma," Jason answered.

"Then let's get them back," Sky said as she walked toward the woods and let out a whistle. At that moment, other vampires came out of the woods, including Mya.

"Umm, Jason," Henry said as he looked around at them.

"Don't worry. I'm kind of their leader. Well, I will be," Sky said as she looked at Jason and Henry. Sky then grabbed Jason's hand, and they all walked into the woods.

Mya walked up to them and stayed close to Sky. They seemed to have walked forever. "So why couldn't you kiss me again the other night? Were you scared you would eat me?" Jason asked with a little laugh. Sky turned and looked at Jason.

"Really… no… when our emotions are high, we can't control our looks. You would have seen my fangs and my eyes, and then you would have known what I was," Sky said.

"Well, you don't have to hide it now," Jason said.

"Stop… do you smell that?" Mya asked.

Everyone stopped, and Sky ran over to Mya. "Yes, I do. I need half to go that way and half to go that way. Mya and I will stay with Jason and Henry," Sky said as she pointed to which way for the vampires to go.

"What do we do if they run toward us?" The other vampires asked. Sky looked at Jason.

"Kill them," Jason said. Sky gave them a nod of approval, and everyone ran to their post. Jason led the way into the den. Sky squeezed Jason's hand very tightly and stopped, which made Jason stop. He turned to look at Sky, and she had her fangs and her eyes were bright red. He knew something was wrong. "Are you ok?" Jason asked.

"I smell a lot of blood… more than your grandma and sister would have. This is a feeding ground," Sky said.

"Stay behind us," Mya said as she walked up beside Sky. As they got closer, they could hear talking.

"Why did you attack them? You didn't have my approval. They will be after us now."

"You got that right," Sky said as they walked around the corner and saw the leader standing there and had a vampire crouched in front of her. "This can get very messy or you can give back the people you took," Mya said.

"Took?" The leader said as she looked back at her guy on the ground in front of her.

"I'm sorry… please don't kill me… we just wanted vengeance," the vampire said.

"Vengeance? Who could you need vengeance against?" The leader asked.

"The hunter." The vampire answered.

"A hunter? You can't be serious! So you attacked a pure-blood warlock and a hunter, which you then took hostages. Are you out of your mind?" The leader asked.

"No… no… we only took one… she is still alive… we didn't know they would find us," The vampire said.

"Where is the one you took?" The leader asked as she grabbed him by the throat.

"In the north den. This is hers… I took it from her neck," The vampire said as he held out Evelyn's neckless. The leader took it and held it out for Jason and the others to take. Jason started to walk up to get it but was stopped by Sky. She then gave Mya a look, and

Mya went to get the necklace. "Take this with you, and whoever is watching the den should let you pass… then tell them to come see me. Apparently, I need to remind them who makes the decisions around here," The leader said.

Mya slowly walked back to Sky. Sky took the necklace and smelled of it to pick up the scent. "This way," Sky said as she led the others to the north den.

The closer they got the stronger the smell. "We are almost there," Sky said. Mya stopped and turned around really fast.

"Did you hear that?" Mya asked as she grabbed Sky.

"Yes! Let's go… Stay here," Sky said as she looked at Jason and kissed him. Mya and Sky then ran into the darkness of the woods.

"Did they really leave us here… in the middle of the woods?" Henry asked.

"Just wait, Henry… they will be back," Jason said.

"Yeah, says your vampire girlfriend," Henry said with a smart mouth. Jason turned and looked at Henry with an aggravated look. He then saw something running up behind Henry.

"Duck Henry!" Jason yelled. Henry dropped to the ground as fast as he could, and Jason threw the person into the tree behind him. "Run… come on… there are too many here, and we can't see," Jason said.

"You can't," Henry said as he stood up and his eyes were glowing. "I can see… stay behind me," Henry said. Jason got right behind Henry so he could lead them toward the den. Henry stopped, reached behind him, and grabbed Jason.

"What is it?" Jason said.

"Don't move. We are very much outnumbered. We need to find a way to get into the cave without being seen," Henry said.

"How many are there?" Jason asked.

"At least 14! We won't make it," Henry said. Suddenly, there was a noise behind them. As the boys turned around, four vampires were standing behind them. "Turn around and walk," The vampires said.

"We were sent here by your leader to get the two you kidnapped," Henry said.

"We only took one, and she is unavailable at the moment…now walk," The vampires said. Jason and Henry didn't have a choice. There were too many and just them, so they had to do what they said. As they walked closer, they could hear the others talking, and they knew who Jason was.

"You Jason… I knew your mom… she didn't like me much, but don't worry, the feeling was mutual. Heard she got trapped by a hunter… is that true?" The vampire asked.

"Where is my grandma and my sister?" Jason asked.

"Oh, was that your family? My bad! Guess we should just say sorry and leave," The vampire said while laughing. He continued, "Or we could just kill you both and keep the old lady for food."

"Where is Ava?" Henry yelled as he ran toward the vampire.

The vampires behind him ran up and grabbed Henry. "Well, that's not nice. You don't yell at people when you visit them. I guess we need to teach you both some manners," the vampire said as he opened his mouth, showed his fangs, and walked toward Henry. Sky came running out of the woods, jumped on the vampire, bit a chunk out of his neck, and then staked him.

"Anyone else?" Sky asked as the other vampires that were with her came out of the woods. Mya walked up and handed Sky the necklace.

"Where is the woman that was wearing this? It was given to us by your leader. She is very unhappy with you all," Sky said.

"We are going into the cave. Do not follow us," Jason said as he started walking to the cave.

"Keep watch," Sky said to Mya as she followed Jason and Henry into the cave.

It was very dark inside, and Jason was the only one that couldn't see. Henry walked in front and Sky was holding Jason's hand to lead his way. "Evelyn!" Henry yelled.

"Take me to her, Sky, please," Jason requested to Sky.

She took both of Jason's hands and took him to Evelyn. Jason grabbed her hand. "Grandma, are you ok?" Jason asked.

"Jason, is that you?" Evelyn asked.

"She is weak! They were feeding on her," Sky suspected.

"We need to get her out of here," Jason said.

"Wait… Jason, if a vampire feeds on a witch, it makes them pretty much immortal for like an hour," Sky warned.

"What do you mean immortal?" Jason asked.

"Very hard to kill. Their wounds heal very quickly, and stakes won't kill them," Sky explained.

"That means the one you killed," Henry said and was interrupted by a lot of yelling outside the cave.

"Get her out of here. Don't you come back for me!" Sky said as she kissed him goodbye.

"Jason Ava isn't here. We have to find her," Henry said.

"We will, but let's get grandma out of here… hold onto me," Jason said. Henry grabbed Jason's arm as he picked up Evelyn and Jason traveled them back to the truck. He handed the keys to Henry.

"Take her home! I'm going back," Jason said.

"No, Jason. You heard what Sky said," Henry said.

"I can't just leave her. Would you leave Ava?" Jason asked. Henry just looked at Jason because he didn't know what to say. He knew he wouldn't leave Ava if she was there.

"That's what I thought," Jason said as he ran back into the woods. Henry jumped in the driver's seat and drove as fast as he could home. Jason was almost back to the cave when he saw someone running toward him. He put his hand out and was just about to throw them.

"Wait! Stop Jason, it's me," Mya said.

"Where is Sky?" Jason asked.

"We got separated. The vampires are stronger than us. I don't know what to do," Mya said.

"Were you leaving? You can't just run from the fight," Jason said.

"No, I was coming to find you. I have an idea… but I don't know if you're going to like it," Mya said as she grabbed his hand, and they ran to find Sky. As they got closer to the cave, they found Sky.

"I told you to run! hy did you come back?" Sky asked.

"Do you really need to ask?" Jason said as he hugged her. "What was your idea?" Jason asked as he looked at Mya.

"They are stronger than us, right? We need to get stronger, too." Mya said.

"No! We are not doing that!" Sky said.

"Doing what?" Jason asked.

"Nothing! It's not an option." Sky answered.

"I would still like to know," Jason said.

Jason looked at Mya, "I was thinking we could take a little of your blood… not much… just a drop is all we need."

"Yes! It's better than everyone getting killed," Jason said.

"No! We are not doing that," Sky said as she walked off. "I have my own idea," Sky said as she held out her hand for Jason. She then took them to the leader again.

"Your vampires are out of control. They have fed on witches. We can't stop them," Sky said. The leader looked up at Sky.

"Where are they?" The leader asked.

"North den," Sky answered. The leader took off to the den. Sky, Jason, and Mya followed her. As they ran up to the cave there was a battle going on.

"Stop!" The leader yelled. Everyone stopped and looked at her, including the one Sky tried to kill.

"What are you doing? You're all acting like animals. We moved back to be home and live in peace. Apparently, we need to leave again. When I took over as leader I said this would be in the past. Now I have to clean up your mess. Let them go," The leader said.

All of Sky's vampires ran to her. "Go home," Sky said.

"I'm sorry this happened to you. You're all free to leave," the leader said as she turned to Jason.

Mya, Sky, and Jason walked back toward the road. "You should head home," Sky said as she hugged Mya.

"I will call you when I get there," Mya said as she ran into the dark woods.

"I smell blood," Sky said as she was trying to figure out where the smell was coming from.

"It's you, Jason. You're hurt," Sky said, and she grabbed Jason and made him sit down.

"I'm ok. It's just a small cut. It doesn't even need stitches," Jason said as he put his hand on Sky's face and kissed her. Henry pulled up as they were starting to get up.

"Where is my grandma?" Jason asked.

"She is safe at home. Are you ok?" Henry asked.

"No, he is not… he got cut," Sky said in an angry voice.

"I'm fine, I promise," Jason said as he laughed a little.

"We need to find Ava. Did the vampires tell you where she was?" Henry asked.

"They don't have her. Let's head back to the farm, and we will figure something out," Jason said.

They all got in the truck and headed to the farm. As they pulled up, Michael ran outside. "Where is Ava?" Michael asked.

"They didn't have her," Henry said.

"we will find her dad. Don't worry," Jason said. He continued, "The leader actually isn't that bad. It was just some vampires from her group were acting alone. She put a stop to it and made them give us grandma and let us go."

"So what do we do about Ava?" Henry asked. At that moment, Sky's phone rang. Everyone stayed quiet while she listened to whoever was talking. Sky looked over to Jason with a furious yet worried look. As Sky hung up, she sat down on the couch.

"I know where Ava is," Sky said.

"What… where… and how did you find out?" Henry asked. Sky looked up at them.

"She is with my brother," Sky said.

"Mike? Are you for real? Did he just like kidnap her or something?" Jason asked.

"I will kill him," Henry said as he ran out the door.

CHAPTER 8

Here it is four days after the party. It's three in the morning, and Ava is still gone. Henry has run off to kill Mike and Jason still can't find him. Sky and Jason are on their way to Sky's house, where they hope Mike is. "If he is there and Henry finds him first, I don't know what Henry will do. He loves Ava and will kill for her if he has to," Jason said.

"Mike just turned sixteen as well and has a lot of anger built up, but I don't think he will hurt her. He is always talking about her, so there is a chance he might like Ava. I honestly don't think he would come here and take her just to hurt her. Besides, he is like me. We only drink from bags," Sky said.

"Oh, that's just great, so now I have two guys that want to be with my sister and how are you both 16?" Jason asked.

"He is my stepbrother," Sky answered as they pulled up at Sky's house. They could hear people yelling.

"We might be too late," Jason said as they ran inside. As they ran into the living room, they saw Ava sitting on the couch, and Mya and Mike were arguing across the room. Jason walked up to Mike.

"Bubba, he didn't hurt me. He cares about me and was scared I would get hurt," Ava said as she jumped up and grabbed Jason by the hand. Jason looked at her for a minute and then hugged her.

"Don't you ever do that again without telling me where she is," Jason said as he turned and looked at Mike.

"You need to leave Mike. Henry is on his way, and he plans to kill you," Sky added.

"I am not scared of that dog. I'm not going anywhere," Mike said.

"Yes, you are. If you hurt him, I won't forgive you," Ava said as she walked up to Mike and grabbed his hand. Mike just looked at her with a soft sad look and started to walk to the door just as the door flew open and Henry walked in. His eyes were glowing from the light, and his claws and fangs were out. He slowly started walking toward Mike.

"Hey man, I'm sorry… I just wanted her to be safe… I wouldn't hurt Ava. I care about her," Mike said as he started backing up. He couldn't fight Henry because Ava asked him not to. Ava finally stepped in between them, and Henry stopped.

"Stop Henry… he didn't hurt me. He was scared for me… please just take me home." Ava said as she walked up and hugged Henry. Everyone was hushed for a minute because they weren't sure what would happen. Henry wrapped his arms around Ava and pulled her very close.

"I was so scared, Ava. I thought I lost you. I would die if something bad happened to you," Henry said and then kissed Ava.

"Will I see you later?" Jason asked before he kissed Sky goodbye.

"Yes, and again, I'm sorry about your sister," Sky said. Jason just smiled as he walked out behind Henry and Ava.

While in the truck on the way home, Jason realized what day it was. "Well, today is your birthday Ava. What do you want to do?" Jason asked.

"I just want to be home with my family," Ava replied.

"You're turning fifteen, Ava… there has to be something you want to do," Jason said.

She just sat quietly for a moment, "I want to go riding like we used to. I miss those days."

As they pulled up at the house, everyone came running out to see Ava. Michael wrapped her in a big hug, picked her up, and asked, "I was so worried about you. Are you ok? Did they hurt you?"

"No, Dad, I'm fine," Ava said. As he sat her down Evelyn was there for the next hug.

"I'm going to get the horses ready," Jason said as everyone started heading inside. Ava smiled at him and walked inside.

"Is Jason taking you riding?" Evelyn asked.

"Yes! He asked me what I wanted for my birthday, and I told him to go riding like we used to," Ava responded.

"Well, that sounds like a great idea," Evelyn said as she kissed Ava's forehead. They all sat in the living room.

"So did Mike," Michael said before being cut off.

"I don't want to talk about it. I'm fine, and I'm home. That's it," Ava said. Evelyn looked at Michael with a worried look. "I just want to go riding. I'm going to see if Jason is ready with the horses." Ava said as she got up and walked toward the door.

"Do you want me to go with you?" Henry asked as he jumped up to follow her.

"No! I just want to spend some time with my brother. We don't get to do that very much anymore." Ava said.

"I understand! Let me walk you to the barn," Henry said as he opened the door for Ava.

As they walked into the barn, Jason was walking up with the two horses, "Are we ready to go?" Jason asked.

"Yes, please," Ava said with a big smile. She then kissed Henry goodbye, got on the horse, and followed Jason from the barn. They took the dirt road to the top of the big heel by their farm. The two stopped at the peak of the hill overlooking the farm. Everything looked so peaceful and beautiful. The sun was coming up, and you could see the whole farm from that spot, including the large pond that seemed to sparkle as the sun beamed across it. Ava had so much on her mind she wanted to talk about. She turned to see Jason looking out at the farm and turned her focus back to the pond.

"Would it be bad if I told Henry we should just be friends?" Ava asked as she looked back out at the farm.

"Why? Are you mad at him?" Jason asked as he turned to look at his sister.

"No, it's just I know he put himself in danger tonight. Well, twice, actually. I just don't want him getting hurt because of me," Ava said as she turned to look at him.

"Well, Ava, the only one who can make that decision is you. Just know whatever you choose, I will support you," Jason said as he grabbed her hand.

"I love you, brother," Ava said with a smile as she looked back down at the farm. Jason smiled at her. He couldn't believe how big his little sister was getting. How grown up she looked on her horse, looking down on the farm. He knew she was going to have her own opinion from now on and that all he could do was protect her and give her support. "I will race you back," Ava said as she looked at Jason with a big smile.

"You're on; let's take the trail," Jason said as he took off on his horse. Ava passed him up and was in the lead as she went around a corner on the trail. As Jason went around the corner, he almost ran into Ava. Jason pulled back as fast as he could to stop the horse, and it threw him onto the ground beside Ava.

"What are you doing, Ava? You could have gotten hurt," Jason said as he stood up and looked at Ava. She was looking in front of her and didn't even notice Jason. As he turned, he saw the vampire leader lying across the trail. She was covered in blood and seemed to be hurt. Jason ran to her. "Are you ok? What happened to you?" Jason asked.

"They are coming," She said before passing out.

"We need to take her home," Jason said.

"Who is that Jason?" Ava asked.

"It's the leader of the vampires that took grandma," Jason answered.

"Wait… what. What did I miss?" Ava asked.

"Too much to explain right now," Jason said. He used his powers to lift the vampire and put her on his horse and then jumped up to hold her. "Move, Ava, as fast as you can," Jason said as the two ran as fast as they could on their horse.

"Henry!" Jason yelled as they got to the house. Henry came running out.

"What? Who is that?" Henry asked.

"It's the leader," Jason said as he got down off the horse. "Help me take her inside," Jason said as he grabbed her and started bringing her down off the horse. Henry then grabbed her under her arms while Jason grabbed the legs, and they carried her inside. Ava came running in behind them. "Can you take the horses to the barn Branson?" Jason asked.

"What happened to her?" Michael asked.

"I'm not sure… all she said was they are coming," Jason said.

"That doesn't sound good. Ava, go to your room, please," Evelyn ordered.

"No… I'm sorry, Grandma, but I'm not a little girl anymore, and I'm not going to hide every time there is danger." Ava said.

"Jason," Evelyn said as she gave him a look as if he was supposed to help make Ava go to her room. Jason just looked at Ava.

"Sorry, grandma… she is right. She is growing up. I have to support her choices. Besides, she is safer around all of us," Jason supported Ava. They walked the leader into the house.

"Henry, call Sky," Jason said. Evelyn brought a bowl of water and a rag to Jason so he could get some of the blood off the leader. She started to wake up, and he was worried she would pass out again, so he had to get as many answers as he could while she was awake. "What happened to you? And who is coming?" Jason asked.

She turned her head slowly and could barely speak. "They tried to kill me. They are coming," The leader said before passing out again.

Henry came running into the room. "Sky is on her way," Henry informed.

"Is she going to be ok?" Ava asked.

"She will be fine; Sky will tell us what to do when she gets here," Jason said.

"Let's just let her rest," Evelyn said.

Suddenly, Sky ran through the door. "Where is she?" Sky asked in a worried voice.

"Over here," Jason answered.

Sky ran to the couch and kneeled beside it. "Oh my God, she is in really bad shape; if she doesn't eat, she is going to die," Sky said.

"She said they tried to kill her and that they are coming," Jason said.

"When a leader is challenged and loses, the leader also loses her or his position as leader. The new leader can then order her or him to follow, or they can order the others to kill him or her. I think she was challenged and lost since the others were drinking Evelyn's blood and were very strong, and they thought she would come here, so they tried to kill her," Sky said.

"So now they are coming after us all," Henry said.

"They will get in; they did last time. Jason, we need more help," Ava said as she looked at Sky.

"I can bring my pack; they will help you," Sky said.

"But first, she needs to eat so she can be strong enough to help," Branson said.

"I will go home and grab some blood," Sky said as she stood up.

"No! I know what she needs," Jason said as he grabbed Sky's arm before she could run off. He pulled his jacket off and held out his wrist.

"NO!" Sky yelled, and she grabbed his hand.

"They drank Evelyn's blood, and she is only half; could you imagine how strong she will be with my blood? We have to do this, and you need to drink it too," Jason said as he turned and looked at Sky. He held out his arm to Sky. "Drink Sky; I will be fine, and this way, I know you will be too," Jason said. Sky looked at him for a minute.

"I really don't want to," Sky said. Jason was getting aggravated and pulled his knife out and cut his wrist, and blood dripped out. Sky turned her face fast away from Jason.

"Don't hide yourself from me, Sky. It doesn't bother me." Jason said. Sky slowly turned back to Jason and grabbed his hand and arm and started to drink. After a minute, the leader woke as she smelled the blood. Sky released Jason's arm.

"Let her drink. She needs it more than I do," Sky said as she pushed his arm to the leader. They raised her head and put his wrist in her mouth, and she grabbed his arm tightly, which hurt Jason a little.

"Ow, not so tight; she is going to break my arm. SOMEONE GET HER OFF!" Jason yelled. Sky grabbed her hands and pulled them from Jason's arms. She looked at Jason with a hungry look.

"I will feed you, but be careful. We want to help you fight back, but to do that, I need to be in one piece," Jason said. He moved his arm back in front of her, and she slowly drank from his wrist and then pushed it away.

"The guy that was calling all the shots behind my back has a bunch of followers. His name is Dan. He told me they were going to kill your family, and I told him we were not murderers, and he said you mean you're not. We are. We don't want to hide in the shadows anymore, and we are going to fix the problem. I tried to tell him it's not about hiding, that it's about survival, but he just wouldn't listen. He grabbed me and bit my neck, and then the others attacked. I managed to get free, and I ran here. I know they are coming," The leader said.

"What is your name?" Jason asked.

"Iris. Thank you for your help," Iris said.

"They will be coming for her and us. We need to get everyone here. We have to figure everything out before they come," Jason said as he stood up.

"I will call Mya and tell her to bring everyone over. Jason, I know there is bad blood between you two, but he is strong and could help. He also really cares about Ava," Sky said as she looked over at Henry.

"You mean Mike, right," Henry confirmed.

"He could help Henry. We need him," Jason said as he looked over at Henry.

"I know, but it doesn't mean I have to like it," Henry said as he took Ava's hand.

"I will tell him to behave. He won't start any trouble; I will make sure of it," Sky reassured. Jason looked at Henry and Ava, and both shook their head yes.

"Call them, but tell Mike if he gets out of line he answers to me," Jason said. Sky went to the other room to call Mya.

"Well looks like I should stick around for a bit," Branson said.

"Might not be a bad idea," Michael said.

"So Sky is a vampire," Branson said.

"Yes, she is a vampire. She also saved our lives. She doesn't feed on live people, and none of her pack does either." Jason said.

Sky walked back into the room and went over to Jason. "They are coming. Mya is calling in everyone. We will have a lot of vampires here if you are ok with that," Sky said as she put her arm around Jason. Jason slid his arm around her and looked at his family.

"We need a lot of help. They follow Sky. She is their leader. They won't do anything unless she says so," Jason said as he looked around the room.

"I trust you. You protected my grandson when he needed you. You are welcome here anytime," Evelyn said as she walked up and hugged Sky.

Ava ran to hug her, too. "Thank you for saving my brother," Ava said.

"I would do it again in a heartbeat. Your brother is pretty special," Sky said as she looked up at Jason. He just smiled at all of them.

"Let's go talk," Jason said as he looked down at Sky. The two walked outside and sat down on the steps.

"So now that I know about you, can you tell me what you and your brother were fighting about? I'm assuming it had to do with vampire things, and that's why you couldn't tell me before," Jason said.

"Well, to be honest, it was about us. Your kind kills my kind. We are actually forbidden to be together. I have liked you for a long time, though, and when you asked me out, I couldn't say no," Sky said as she looked at the ground.

"I wouldn't hurt you. Did Mike think I would?" Jason asked.

"He is worried about what my mom will think, but honestly, I don't think she is coming back. We haven't heard from her in a while," Sky said as she looked at Jason.

"I will help you find her if you want me to when this is over," Jason said as he hugged her. Ava and Henry walked out the door and joined them on the steps.

"So what's the plan?" Henry asked.

"We protect the family and kill them all if we have to," Jason said as he held Sky close.

"The whole family," Ava said as she grabbed Sky's hand. Sky smiled at her. They were a weird family but that's what they were. They sat there for a little longer, and then Sky looked out into the trees and stood up quickly.

"They are here," Sky said.

"Took them long enough," Henry said.

"No… Not them, Henry; her pack. GET IN THE HOUSE NOW!" Sky yelled. They all ran into the house, and Jason shut the door and locked it. "They are already here," Sky said.

"I don't understand. Why would they come during the day; they see better than us at night and that would be their advantage," Branson said. Everyone stood there thinking for a minute.

"They are here for me," Iris said as she stood up.

"You're not going out there," Jason said.

"If I don't, they are going to attack your home," Iris said.

"No… No one else is going to die," Jason paused. "Except them," Henry continued.

"Besides, didn't you say they wanted to kill us anyways? If you go out there and they kill you, then that's just one less person on our side," Jason said.

"I just have one question: who are these people?" Ava asked. Everyone turned to look at Ava. "I will fill her in," Henry said as he grabbed her hand and sat her down.

They were all sitting and waiting for the vampires to attack, but for some reason, they stayed at the edge of the farm. "I don't understand what they are waiting for," Branson said.

"I need to run upstairs to the bathroom. I will be right back," Ava said.

"You are not going alone. I will walk with you," Henry said. He grabbed Ava's hand and walked her upstairs. She walked into the bathroom and closed the door. She listened carefully against the door to make sure Henry wasn't too close. She pulled out her phone to text Mike. No one knew she had his number yet and she didn't want Henry to find out after everything that happened that morning.

"You need to get here quick. The other vampires are here, and I know they want to kill my brother. If you really care about me, you will come protect him. Bring everyone." Ava wrote in a text.

"Are you ok, Ava?" Henry asked.

"Yes, I will be right out; just washing up a little," Ava said as she put her phone back in her pocket, grabbed a washcloth, and started washing her face. She opened the door, and Henry was standing there. He brushed her hair from her face and kissed her.

"I can't believe I almost lost you earlier," Henry said.

"He wasn't going to hurt me; he's actually really sweet. He told me he loved going to the party with me, and if he was smart, he would have asked me out that night," Ava said as she stepped back and turned away from him. It bothered her that everyone was so mean to Mike when he was so nice to her. He protected her, and in her own way, she kind of liked him. She didn't want to like him because she loved Henry, but she couldn't stop thinking about Mike.

"You ready to go back downstairs with the others?" Henry said as he walked up and put his hands around her waist.

"Yes," Ava said as she walked out the door without looking at him. He followed her back down to the others and walked over to Jason as Ava went to the kitchen.

"I think your sister is falling for Mike," Henry said as he looked at Jason.

"That's crazy; she loves you," Jason said.

"Well, she just defended Mike and got very tense and upset with me when I mentioned what he did," Henry said as he looked at Ava in the kitchen. Jason turned to look at Ava as well, and she turned to see them looking at her and turned away.

"I will talk to her later. I will figure out what's going on," Jason said. He couldn't help but think about her question earlier.

"What if she asked me? Would it be bad if I told Henry we should just be friends because she wanted to break up with Henry and date Mike?" Jason thought to himself.

He must have been lost in thought because his dad was talking to him, and he didn't hear him, "SON! Are you ok? I have called your name like three times."

"Yes, sorry was just lost in thought," Jason said. At that moment, Sky's phone started ringing in the kitchen. She ran to pick it up and walked into the living room.

"Hang on, I'm putting you on speaker," Sky said as she sat the phone down on the coffee table.

"Hey, what's going on?" Jason questioned.

"We are outside the farm and they have the place surrounded. I don't think we can get through without being seen. What do you want us to do?" Mya asked. Jason looked at Sky and waited for her to respond. "Hello, are you still there, Jason?" Mya asked.

"You're asking me?" Jason asked. "Yes; Sky said for us to follow you. We are fully ready to fight on your command," Mya said. Jason looked around the room.

"I have a better idea. Pick a few of your best fighters and go to the big pine tree by the pond. Tell the others to surround the other vampires but not to be seen and wait till the fighting starts," Jason said.

"Got it. I will send a text when the groups are made," Mya said.

"I am going to get the best fighters. I will travel them all here to fight with us, and as the pack closes in on us, then Sky's pack can close in from behind and surprise them," Jason said.

"That is a lot of people to travel, Jason. It could hurt you," Ava said.

"I have to try Ava. They need to be here with us for this plan to work, and the other pack isn't going to let them walk in." Jason said in an aggravated voice. Ava turned away and ran upstairs. She ran into her room and slammed and locked the door and then locked the bathroom door so no one could get into her room. She pulled out her phone to text Mike again and saw a text from him.

"I was already on my way. I found a way to sneak through the vampires, and I'm in your barn," Mike said in his text.

"I'm about to sneak out and come to you," Ava replied.

"No, do not do that. It's not safe out here. I want you to stay inside around people that can keep you safe," Mike replied.

"Well, I'm not exactly around people. I have locked myself in my room, away from everyone. I am just really sad and scared. All Jason wants to do is run straight into danger, and all Henry wants to do is talk about what happened this morning as if I almost died. I just want to cry, but I'm even too scared to do that," Ava replied.

"Do you want me to make you smile because I can do that?" Mike replied with a smiley face.

"How are you going to do that?" Ava replied.

"Look out your window," Mike replied. Ava walked over to her curtain to look out toward the barn, and as she pulled the curtain back, she saw Mike standing on the roof in front of her window.

"Oh my God! Did anyone see you? You are crazy if my brother catches you. Oh my God, no, if Henry catches you," Ava said as she was freaking out while removing the board and opening the window.

Mike crawled through her window and stepped up in front of her. He slid his arm around her waist and pulled her into a big hug. As she looked up at him, she smiled. "Told you I could make you smile," Mike said.

"How are we going to explain this?" Ava asked.

"We won't. After I visit with you for a minute I will go back out the window and knock on the front door. No one has to know I was even in here," Mike said as he looked down at her smiling face.

"I can't believe you are here," Ava said as she put her head against his chest and wrapped her arms around his neck.

"Please don't be mad, but I have to do something. Something I should have done the night of the party when I realized just how much I liked you," Mike said as he slid his hands through her hair.

"What are you going to do?" Ava asked as she lifted her head and looked at him. He slowly leaned in and kissed her and then pulled away. She didn't know what to think. She was very quiet and just looked at him.

"I'm sorry. I really shouldn't have done that; I'm going to go. I will see you downstairs," Mike said as he started to turn away.

"Wait; don't leave yet," Ava said as she walked up to him and got very close. "Is there a chance you could hurt me?" Ava asked as she slid her arms around his neck again.

"No chance at all. You're very special to me," Mike said as he leaned in to kiss her again. She could feel how passionate he was with his kiss and she got very passionate herself. He slid his hands down to her legs and picked her up, and she wrapped her legs around him. He took her to the bed and to lie her down gently and never stopped kissing her. She pulled away to breathe for a second, and he could hear her breathing heavily, which made him want to kiss her even more. He started kissing her neck, put his hand against her hip, and pulled her against him.

"We have to stop," Mike said.

"No, we don't," Ava said.

"You're only fifteen, Ava. We need to slow down." Mike argued.

"You're sixteen so that only makes us a year apart; wait, are you a virgin?" Ava asked.

"No, are you?" Mike asked. Ava didn't want to answer. She thought it would make him want to be with someone more experienced. "It doesn't bother me if you are. I really expected you to be. That's why I said we should slow down." Mike said.

"I don't want to wait. I want you," Ava said as she rose up and kissed him. She wrapped her legs around him tightly, and he grabbed her hip and pulled her into him.

"Ava, we shouldn't," Mike said as he felt her pulling herself against him. He finally gave in and grabbed her in a gentle but forceful way and slid his hand around to her back.

Suddenly, there was a knock at the door. "Ava, I'm sorry. Can I come in?" Jason asked.

"IT'S JASON! YOU HAVE TO HIDE," Ava said in a quiet but firm voice. Mike jumped up and started out the window but turned to kiss Ava one more time. She smiled at him before showing him out the window. She walked over to the door slowly to give Mike time to get away.

"I can hear you. Will you please just open the door; if you don't, I'm coming in anyways," Jason said. Ava opened the door.

"What do you want? You made it very clear earlier that your way is the only way to do anything," Ava said.

"I was wrong for snapping at you. I should have said things differently. Do you forgive me?" Jason asked. Jason then saw the window. "Why did you take the board off the window? That's very dangerous, Ava." Jason said just as there was a knock at the door.

"Hide, Ava," Jason said as he ran downstairs. Henry was standing at the bottom of the stairs, waiting to protect her as always. Jason peeked out the small window next to the door.

"What the Hell," Jason said as he opened the door.

"Get inside. How did you get past everyone?" Jason asked.

"I'm sneaky, fast and smart. Unlike some of you," Mike said as he looked at Henry. Everyone looked over at Henry, who was just staring at Mike. He slowly walked over to Mike.

"Stay away from Ava, and there won't be a problem," Henry said in a calm voice and then turned to walk away.

"What's wrong? Scared she will choose someone stronger and faster? Oh, and let's not forget better looking," Mike said, followed by a little laugh.

"I am going to Ava's room to lie down. If you need me, you know where to find me," Henry said as he smiled at Mike and headed up the stairs. Ava heard him and fixed the bed really fast. She didn't need him asking questions. She had just sat down on the bed when Henry walked in.

"Who's here?" Ava asked.

"It's your best friend, Mike," Henry said as he shut the door.

"Really; did you really just say that?" Ava said as she stood up and shoved Henry.

"What is wrong with you, Ava? Why are you acting like this?" Henry asked.

"You and Jason act like Mike tried to kill me. Why don't you two thank him for saving me? Since the vampires took Grandma,

I'm sure they would have taken me, too, if Mike hadn't taken me first. He was very nice to me as well and took care of me," Ava said.

"Nice to you; are you serious, Ava? He kidnapped you," Henry said.

"No… Actually, he didn't. When we got outside the farm he stopped and asked if I was ok. He said he heard them saying to get the girl, and he thought they were coming for me, so he came and got me first. He asked if I wanted him to take me back, and I said no. I was too scared to come home, and I knew I would just be in the way. Then I told him to take me to his house… Now you know the whole story… Look, Henry, I think we should take a break. I'm not sure what I want anymore," Ava said as she opened the door and ran downstairs and out the front door.

"Ava! Come back here!" Jason yelled.

"I will go get her," Mike said.

"No… I will go. She needs a girl to talk to," Sky said as she ran out after her.

"Ava… where are you?" Sky called out.

"I'm in the barn," Ava said in a sad voice. Sky walked in and saw her sitting on some hay and sat down beside her.

"You want to talk about what's bothering you?" Sky asked.

"It's nothing," Ava answered.

"Didn't sound like nothing? Us vamps can hear really well when we are trying," Sky said.

"What did you hear?" Ava asked as she turned to look at Sky.

"Are you asking about Henry or my brother?" Sky asked while looking at her.

"You know about your brother being in my room? Did you hear everything?" Ava asked.

"I heard enough. I didn't tell your brother or anyone, and I won't, but you have to decide what you want. You can't have them both," Sky said as she hugged Ava.

"What if I don't know what I want?" Ava asked.

"Then take the time to decide and tell the boys to wait or move on. You need to be happy, and if they care about you, then they will wait," Sky said. They both sat there for a minute until they heard a noise coming from the back of the barn.

"What was that?" Ava asked as she stood up really fast. Sky jumped up as well and put Ava behind her. Just then, four vampires stepped out of the shadows.

"Look, it's two helpless little girls," The one that seemed to be running the show said.

"And one is just too cute to pass up. You want a vampire boyfriend? Come with me. I will make you happy," one of the guys said as he laughed and winked at her.

"Ava, run and don't stop," Sky said as she pushed her away.

She ran to the door and turned back to see them circling Sky and knew she was going to get hurt so she ran to the house to get the others. As she got closer to the house, she started to yell. "JASON! HENRY! MIKE! SOMEONE HELP!" Ava yelled. Mike heard her and turned toward the door.

"AVA IS IN TROUBLE!" Mike said as he ran out the door, followed by Jason and Henry. They ran to Ava, and Jason grabbed her.

"What's wrong? Are you ok?" Jason asked. She was very out of breath from running so fast but managed to answer.

"The barn, Sky; vampires," Ava said, out of breath. Jason and Mike ran to the barn.

"Take her inside!" Jason yelled to Henry. As they walked inside, the adults were coming into the living room.

"What's going on?" Branson asked.

"She said there are vampires in the barn with Sky," Henry said as he sat her down. Branson grabbed his crossbow and ran outside to the barn to help. As he walked in, he saw Jason standing there with a note, and Mike was throwing hay around the barn in a mad rage.

"What happened?" Branson asked. Jason turned and handed him the note and walked out of the barn before he broke down.

Note: You have something of ours, and now we have something of yours. We will do a fair trade at nightfall. If you don't give us what we want, we will take it out on your poor little princess.

Jason walked back into the house and sat down. "Where is Sky?" Ava asked.

"They took her. They want to trade for Iris," Jason said as he looked at Iris.

"Has this been their plan all along? Have they been waiting to kidnap Sky? Is that why they haven't attacked yet?" Henry asked.

"I don't know Henry. Maybe. I don't understand one thing, though. The note called her a little princess. Why would a vampire call another vampire that?" Jason asked. Ava stood there thinking about what the vampire said and the note.

"They don't call each other that. We usually call each other vamps," Iris said.

Ava remembered Sky saying us vamps earlier in the barn, and then it clicked. The vampire was saying she should come with him earlier. "Jason. They were not after Sky." Ava said as she looked at him. Jason just sat there looking at her as if he was waiting for her to explain.

"The vampire said; well, he told me I should go with him, and then Sky told me to run. I think they were there for me," Ava said.

"That would make sense. She doesn't have magic yet and can't really defend herself, yet her blood is still the blood of a witch, and they could feed on her to get stronger," Iris said.

"They were going to feed on me?" Ava asked in a scared voice as Mike walked in with Branson.

"Wait, they were after Ava?" Mike asked.

"That's what we are thinking. Mike and Henry, come with me for a minute, and let's talk," Jason said as he stood up and started toward the kitchen.

"Let's get you cleaned up," Iris said as she took Ava's hand. Ava pulled away.

"I'm sorry, but I don't trust you yet. I can do it myself," Ava said as she stood up and walked upstairs.

"It will take some time, but she will come around," Evelyn assured.

"I understand. My pack kidnapped you and fed on you. I can understand her not trusting me," Iris said.

The boys were in the kitchen trying to come up with a plan to save Sky without giving Iris to them. "We are not alone in this, and I have to go get the others soon. When I tell them what happened, they might not listen to me," Jason said.

"No, they will. Sky told everyone that you are calling the shots tonight and that if we didn't listen, we would be punished," Mike said.

"Well, that didn't stop you, now did it?" Henry asked with a sarcastic voice.

"Yeah, well, I never listen, so," Mike countered.

"Alright, look, Mike, I need you to call Mya and see if they are ready and I will tell them when I get there. We need them here to get a full plan going," Jason said. Mike walked out to the back porch to call Mya.

"Are we really going to trust vampires to get us out of this fight when we are fighting vampires to begin with?" Henry asked.

"You mean, are we going to trust Mike? Yes, we are because he is strong, and we need his help, like Sky said," Jason said.

At that moment, Mike walked back in and informed, "Mya said they are headed to the tree now but are trying to be careful not to be seen with it still being daylight."

"I should head to the tree then and wait so I can grab them in a hurry if needed. Can I trust you two to get along until I get back?" Jason asked. They both looked at each other, and then Mike walked back to the living room.

"Be nice; we need his help," Jason said as he looked at Henry. Jason then disappeared to head to the tree. As he appeared at the tree, he ducked to hide in case anyone was watching. In the distance, he heard someone call his name very faintly. He started to look around and saw Mya. She was pointing to the other side of the pond, where two vampires were walking by. He crawled over to her so he wouldn't be seen.

"How long have they been there?" Jason asked.

"Not sure; we just got here," Mya said.

"Where are the others?" Jason asked.

"Back this way; follow me and stay down," Mya said. They crawled a little ways through the trees, and then Mya stood up, so Jason did, too.

"We should hurry; in case they plan to come this way; how many did you bring?" Jason asked.

"Seven," Mya said. Jason was just looking at the ground for a minute.

"Is that enough? You said the strongest. They are our strongest fighters," Mya said as she looked at Jason.

"Seven is plenty. I have just never traveled that many people before. Not sure how weak I will be after. We need to go now so I can rest before anything happens," Jason said. Mya rounded up the group and told them how they were getting to Jason's house.

"Everyone grab hands and close your eyes and do not let go no matter what. For those that have never traveled before, it can make you a little queasy after we get where we are going," Jason said.

Everyone grabbed hands, and soon they all disappeared. They made it to the barn and Jason couldn't go any further. When they stopped, Jason collapsed.

"Jason, someone pick him up. We have to get to the house," Mya said. They walked in carrying Jason.

"Oh my God, what happened?" Ava said as she ran to Jason.

"He stopped at the barn. I don't know. He just collapsed. Is he okay?" Mya asked in a troubled voice.

"I knew it was too much," Henry said.

"Put him on the couch and let him rest. He should be up soon," Evelyn said. After they put him on the couch, Mya looked around the room.

"Where is Sky?" Mya asked.

"Jason didn't tell you?" Henry asked.

"Tell me what?" Mya asked as she looked around the room. Henry looked at Mike.

"Sky was kidnapped by the vampires earlier. Jason was supposed to tell you when he got there," Mike said as he walked over to Mya.

"Why are we not trying to get her back?" Mya asked in an angry voice.

"We are. They left a note. They want to trade for Iris," Branson said.

"Who are you?" Mya asked. Mike stepped in between them.

"His name is Branson, and he is a hunter," Mike informed. Mya just looked around the room.

"So we are working with hunters now. They kill our kind. They don't care about us," Mya said.

"He cares. He wants to help. He's after the same vampires we are," Jason said as he was lying on the couch waking up. Everyone rushed over to him.

"Are you okay?" Ava said as she wrapped him in a big hug.

"I will never hurt anyone who has done nothing wrong. Everyone has the right to exist as long as they treat others the same way. Jason saved my life, and for that, I promised to help him with the problems they are having here," Branson said as he put his hand out to shake Mya's hand. She thought about it for a second and then looked at Jason and shook his hand.

"If Jason trusts you, then I guess I do, too," Mya said.

"So what's your idea? Do you have a plan?" Mya asked.

"We need to distract them so we can grab Sky. I can get in without being seen if I travel to her, but they can't be watching," Jason said.

"Jason, you can't travel again right now. It might kill you. You're just way too weak," Ava argued.

"You know what we have to do," Iris said as she looked at Jason.

"No, that's not an option. We are not trading." Jason said.

"Then Sky will die, and they win anyway," Iris said in an aggravated voice.

"There has to be another way without," Jason said before getting cut off. "Look, I want my sister back, and if I have to, I'm going to get her alone, and I will kill anyone who gets in my way," Mike said. Ava stood up and walked over to him.

"Or they will capture you too, and since we only have one person to trade, they will kill the other. We have to be smart. They want Iris, right? Well, let's give her to them," Ava said as she looked around the room.

Jason stood up quickly and was about to say something. "Just hear me out. If she challenges the leader, they have to fight her and win to stay the leader, correct? Well, it's been a while since they fed on grandma, and we have stronger blood than that anyway," Ava said.

"Jason can't feed anyone right now. He's too weak," Evelyn added.

"I wasn't talking about his. I was talking about mine," Ava said.

"Are you out of your mind, Ava? You're not letting vampires feed on you," Jason said.

"Sky fed off of you, and the only reason they took her was because she was very outnumbered. I could feed at least four vampires here, and if they worked together, they could kill them all and get Sky back. We act as if we are going to make the trade, and then Iris could get to Sky and fight their way out, and we could fight our way in. I'm open to any better plans," Ava suggested as she looked at Jason.

Everyone was very quiet. Even the vampires didn't want to say anything. "If we do this I pick the vampires. I know them all better than any of you," Mya said.

"Fine, but I am picking one," Ava said as she walked over to Mike.

"I can't feed on you, Ava," Mike said as he looked at her with sadness.

"You have to if you want to save your sister," Ava said.

"Let's just take a minute, and Mya, you can gather your vampires in case we go with Ava's plan, which isn't likely," Jason said.

"In case? Tell me you're not really considering this. You are going to let them bite her?" Henry asked in an angry voice.

"No, we will find another way. Let's go to my room," Jason said as he looked at Henry.

The boys left the room to go upstairs, and Ava walked over to Evelyn and Michael, who were being very quiet. "I have to do this. You know that, right? I just want to help save everyone, and I don't have my magic yet, so this is all I can do," Ava said as she hugged them both. Evelyn had a tear roll down her cheek. They both smiled at her and left the room. Ava ran over to Iris. "If we do this, will it work?" Ava asked.

"I can't say for sure, but I know it's a chance," Iris said.

"Good enough for me," Ava said as she held out her arm to the others.

"We should wait for Jason," Mya said.

"No. It's my blood, and I decide," Ava said. Mike walked up to her and kissed her. He held her hand as he bit into her arm, and she turned her head away. Mya walked over and drank a little, as well as two other vampires.

"This is Lily. She is from another pack that hunters wiped out and this is Rick; he was turned by your mom long ago," Mya said.

"You knew our mom?" Ava asked as she teared up a little.

"Yes. I'm so sorry to hear what happened. I wish she was alive to see her kids now," Rick said.

"Has no one told you? She is alive. She is in a hunter prison. We are trying to save her," Ava said as she took Rick's hand. He looked so surprised yet angry at the same time. "Whatever you guys are planning to get her back, count me in," Rick said as he hugged Ava.

CHAPTER 9

It was starting to get late, and Jason and Henry were walking back downstairs. "Just for the record, I am not okay with this," Henry said as he looked at everyone.

"Well, it doesn't matter because it's already done," Ava said.

"What do you mean?" Jason asked. Ava held up her arm to show the bandages.

"What did you do? I told you to wait," Jason said.

Evelyn and Michael walked into the room. "It was her choice, Jason," Michael said.

"Oh, sure, now you want to be the perfect dad. Let her do what she wants so she can forgive you for never being there," Jason said.

"Jason, don't talk to him like that. You know why he has been gone," Evelyn said.

"Yes, I do. Chasing something he couldn't even get himself. He had to get his son to do it for him," Jason yelled as he walked to the kitchen, followed by Henry.

"I don't like it either, but it's done. Let's kill these guys and get our life back," Henry said.

"You don't understand Henry. We will never get our lives back," Jason said as he turned to look at him.

Ava walked into the room. "I want to help, and this was the only way I could. I don't want you mad at me, but I had to do it, and you would have stopped me. I feel fine, and now the vampires are stronger, and you need the help," Ava said as she walked up to Jason. He hugged her, and she could tell he was just relieved that she was okay. They all walked back into the living room.

"How does everyone feel?" Jason asked.

Mya, Mike, Rick, and Lily stepped forward. "We are ready to fight," Mya said.

"Wait outside on the front porch and leave the light off so they don't know we have walked outside yet. The light will draw attention," Jason said.

They all started to walk outside, and Ava reached out and grabbed Rick's arm, and he turned to her. "He knew our mother. She turned him with magic," Ava said as she looked at Jason.

"I was very sick and only had months to live, and your mom said she could keep me alive, but there would be a price of drinking from the living. I told her I wanted to live, and she turned me. I owe your mom my life, and I will help you save hers," Rick said as he shook Jason's hand and pulled him into a hug. Jason looked at Ava, who was starting to cry a little. He could tell she finally had hope to see her mother.

"Thank you, Rick. That means a lot. Head outside with the others, and I will be right there," Jason said.

"Henry, you're not going to like this, but I need you with me. Mike, I need you inside to protect my family if anyone gets in this house. My grandma and dad have magic, but they are not full-blood and need spells to cast. It will take too long if too many get in. Work with Branson. He is good at what he does," Jason said as he walked to the door. He turned back to see everyone looking at him then opened the door to step out.

"I got this man. Just save my sister," Mike said. Jason turned back and gave a nod to Mike.

"See you outside, Henry," Jason said as he shut the door.

Just outside, everyone was ducked down. "What's going on?" Jason asked.

"They are close. We have been watching them," Mya said.

"Have you seen Sky?" Jason asked.

"Not yet. We have been watching for her," Mya said.

Jason used his power to talk to Henry inside, "Have them turn the lights out and get out here." Henry was inside telling everyone bye when he heard the message and he turned to the door.

"Turn the lights out. Something is wrong," Henry said as he ran to the living room light switch.

"What? How do you know? I don't hear anything," Mike said as he turned the kitchen light off.

"Jason told me," Henry said as he ran to the door.

"Jason can get into your head," Evelyn said. Henry opened the door, went out, and ducked behind Jason.

"What is going on?" Henry asked.

Jason pointed out into the pasture that was close to the house. "Use your wolf vision and see if you can see Sky," Jason said.

"I can smell her," Henry said as he turned Jason around to talk to him.

"Smell her? Since when did you learn how to do that?" Jason asked.

"Since she has been in your house and I have been around her scent for so long," Henry said. Jason turned back around and looked at Mya. She looked worried.

"What is it?" Jason asked.

"We are very outnumbered, Jason. I don't know what we are going to do," Mya said.

"I can track her, Jason. I can find her. I just need a path," Henry said.

"Mya, you go with Henry. I am going to take the others and make a distraction," Jason said.

"Stay down," Mya said as she grabbed Henry's hand and ran around the side of the house. Jason went to the others behind the bushes.

"Let's start some trouble," Jason said as he looked at them.

"That's our specialty," Rick said as he smiled. The vampires all stood up and ran out into the pasture, yelling. "You want to play let's play. Bring it on, vamps." Rick said. The other vamps started to notice them. They started walking toward them.

"You do realize you are way outnumbered right?" The other vamps asked while laughing.

"You do realize we are on full-blooded witch's blood right?" Rick asked as he ran toward them with a smile. The other vamps stopped and took a few steps back, unsure of what to do, as Rick ran toward them. They turned to run away just a little too late as Rick grabbed one and threw him to the ground. "Where is our leader?" Rick asked.

"Get off of me!" The vamp yelled.

"Sorry, but I only listen to my leader, and I don't see her, do you?" Rick asked with a smart mouth. The other vamps were watching just a few feet away. They were scared to try to help.

"Well, this one isn't talking," Rick said and he put his hand through his chest and pulled his heart out. He took a few steps toward the others and they started to run when suddenly they were all pulled back toward Rick and the others. They turned and looked and realized Jason wouldn't let them leave. Rick ran for the biggest one, grabbed him by the head, and ripped it clean off. "Who's next?" Rick asked in a terrifying voice.

"Stop! We need these ones. They could know something useful," Jason said.

Rick turned to look at him and then looked at the other vamps on their side behind him. "You heard him. Grab them and make them comfortable in the house," Rick said.

"Put them in the basement and tell Mike to watch them and to keep Ava away," Jason said.

The vamps took the two they caught to the house. As they walked in, everyone stepped back. "Who are they?" Ava asked as she stepped behind Mike. Mike put his arm out and stepped in front of Ava.

"Jason told us to bring them inside and put them in the basement. He also said to have you watch them," The vamps said as they looked at Mike. Mike then looked at Branson, and he waited for him to come over to stand with Ava before he walked with the others down stairs. As they got to the basement Mike was looking to see if they had a way out.

"No windows or doors; well, except the one behind me, and good luck getting to that one alive, but I really hope you try. Just give me a reason to rip your head off," Mike said as he sat down on the stairs.

"Jason also told us to tell you to keep Ava away from them," The other vamps said as they walked back up the stairs to head back outside. Mike watched them leave and then turned his focus back to the vampires in the basement.

"Looks like we can have a little talk now. Why does your leader want Ava?" Mike asked.

"Don't tell him anything," The tall one said.

"Not a good idea. It would be in your best interest to answer my questions before your usefulness runs out," Mike said as he looked at the shorter one.

"He," The shorter one said before being cut off.

"SHUT UP!!" The tall one yelled. "He is going to kill us anyway."

"You're probably right, but I could make it fast or painful, and that depends on your answers and I would choose them wisely from now on," Mike said as he looked at them both. They both looked at each other. Neither knew what to do at this point. "I'm ok with either choice so please make up your mind fast so we can figure this out. Now same question; what does your leader want with Ava?" Mike asked again. Just about that time, Ava walked down the stairs behind him.

"I would like to know the answer to that question," Ava said.

"Ava, you can't be down here," Mike said as he stood up in front of her.

"I can't just stay up there knowing they are down here. Besides, he's one of the vamps that grabbed Sky," Ava said as she pointed to the tall one. Mike turned to look at him, and they could see the anger on his face. He ran to the vamp and grabbed him.

"Where is my sister? I should kill you right now," Mike said as he put his hand around the vamp's neck. Ava ran to him to stop him before he killed him.

"STOP! MIKE STOP YOU WILL KILL HIM!" Ava yelled while pulling on his arm.

"You say that like it's a bad thing," Mike said as he stared the vamp in the eye. Just about that time, the shorter vamp grabbed Ava and wrapped her in his arms with his fangs out, and was about to bite her neck when an arrow came flying from nowhere and hit him in the shoulder. He instantly let Ava go, and Mike grabbed her.

"Good thing I came to look at the zoo animals," Branson said as he came the rest of the way down the stairs.

"Are you ok?" Mike asked.

"Yes, can you just take me back upstairs?" Ava asked as she started walking toward the stairs.

"You don't even know who you are, do you?" The taller vamp asked as he looked at Ava

"What do you mean? I'm Ava," Ava answered.

"Yea, just Ava? You should ask why you were of interest to us. Someone in this house knows," The taller vamp said as he laughed. Mike turned her around and started walking up the stairs. He stopped and turned to Branson.

"If they even look at you funny, shoot them," Mike said. Branson patted him on the shoulder and sat down to watch them.

As they stepped out upstairs, Evelyn was sitting there with her necklace, talking to someone. "Who are you talking to?" Ava asked.

"This necklace lets me have short conversations with your mother," Evelyn said as she grabbed Ava's hand.

"Ava is here with me now," Evelyn said.

"Ava, my sweet daughter. I miss you so much and can't wait to hold you in my arms," Emma said.

Ava started to cry. "I have always wondered what your voice sounds like. Oh, Mom, I love you so much," Ava said as she cried even more.

"We have some of them held captive in the basement. Hopefully, we will get answers soon," Evelyn said.

"Mom, one said I need to ask who I am, and that would explain why they want me," Ava said.

"Just do what grandma says, and everything will be fine," Emma said as Evelyn let go of Ava. Ava could see that Evelyn was listening to her mother.

"Why did you let go? What is she saying?" Ava asked.

"Don't worry, they will be fine, and we will talk to them as soon as we get you back," Evelyn said as she let go of her locket. She turned to Ava and wrapped her in a hug. "I know you and your brother will have lots of questions when everything calms down, but let's wait till we get your mother back to talk about it," Evelyn said. Ava wanted answers now and was very upset that her grandmother wouldn't answer her. She turned away and walked out of the room. Mike followed her closely behind as she headed for the basement door.

"Ava! You can't go down there," Mike said as he grabbed her hand to stop her.

"I'm getting answers. Something is going on, and if they won't tell me, the vamp downstairs might," Ava said as she pulled away. Michael stepped in front of her to stop her.

"Why are you trying to go back down there?" Michael asked.

"We need to talk to you," Mike said. They all sat down in the living room, and Ava calmly told her dad everything.

Mya and Henry were still making their way through the vampires unseen as they were all distracted by the others. "I can smell her. She is close. Let's move this way," Henry said as he moved past the bushes. He turned around to see Mya didn't follow.

"Mya? Mya? Where are you?" Henry whispered. Just about that time, a vamp grabbed him, and before he could do anything, Mya jumped on his back, broke his neck, and pulled his head off. As he fell, Mya landed on her feet.

"I understand you want to find Sky, and so do I, but we need to be careful. He watched you sneak out of the bushes and came for you, so I hid to wait. Keep your head in this, or we will die," Mya said as she looked up at Henry.

"Thanks. That was close," Henry said.

"Follow me and stay low," Mya said. Henry ducked down behind her and followed her. As they got closer to the camp, Henry could smell Sky, and the scent was very strong.

"I think she is in this tent," Henry whispered as he grabbed Mya's hand. Mya looked at her hand, gave him a nod, and took out a knife. She put a small cut in the tent to peek through. She saw Sky sitting there, and she looked very weak.

"You were right. She is in there. I'm going to get her. Stay here," Mya said as she let go of his hand and walked around the side of the tent. As she got inside, she could smell something strange. She looked over and found a needle and then a bottle that said morphine on it. "They drugged her? You have got to be kidding me," Mya thought to herself. "Sky, wake up! Sky, come on, it's time to leave. Snap out of it," Mya said as she was tapping and shaking her to try and wake her up.

Another vamp walked in behind her but she didn't hear him because she was trying to wake up Sky. As the vamp was about to grab her, Henry ran in, tackled him to the ground, and wrapped his hands around his neck. "Don't touch her," Henry said as he squeezed tighter. It scared Mya, and she jumped back till she realized what had happened, and then she ran to Henry.

"Let him go. He's out. I need you to help me grab Sky. She's been drugged," Mya said as she walked back over to Sky. Henry let him go and ran to Sky.

"Let's get her out of the camp and call Jason. He can come to travel us out of here," Henry said. They picked her up and slowly walked out of the tent and back into the woods. Henry grabbed his phone and called Jason. "We have her. She's been drugged, and we can't fight and carry her. We need you to come get us," Henry said.

"Tell me where you are," Jason said.

"We are in the big clearing of the field," Henry said.

"Alright, hold tight," Jason said as he hung up. They hid in the tall grass, waiting for Jason. Jason ran back to the house to tell everyone about Sky. As he ran in, he saw Ava, Michael, and Mike sitting on the couch. They turned to look at him. "They found Sky. I'm going to get them," Jason informed.

"How are you going to get them?" Ava asked.

"You can't travel, Jason your still too weak," Michael said. Evelyn heard them from the kitchen and came into the room.

"We can't stop him every time. He has to learn to control his powers and find his weakness," Evelyn interrupted.

"I will be careful, but I have to try," Jason said as he looked at Ava and disappeared.

As Jason appeared and didn't see them, he used his mind to let Henry know he was there. Henry stood up as soon as he heard him. Jason saw them about ten feet in front of him and ran to them. "What did they give her?" Jason asked.

"Morphine, and she is very weak because of it. I can't even wake her up," Mya said.

Jason wrapped her in his arms and tried to wake her. "Sky, it's me, Jason. Can you open your eyes for me?" Jason asked.

Sky tried to look at him so hard, but her head fell back again. She was way too out of it to know what was happening. "We need to get her to Evelyn. She will know what to do," Henry offered.

"There is only one problem. I think I can only carry one," Jason said as he looked at Henry and Mya. They looked at each other and could read each other's faces.

"Take her and go. We can fight our way back if we have to and it would be easier since we wouldn't have Sky to protect," Mya said.

Jason looked down at Sky and then back at them, "Be careful, and if anything happens, I will try to come back," Jason said before he disappeared. Mya and Henry headed back toward the house as soon as he was gone. They knew it would take a while because as soon as they noticed Sky was gone, they would come looking for whoever took her.

"Let's cross the trail and go to the other side of the farm. They will expect us to go straight to the house and won't find us so quickly," Henry said.

Mya looked at him. "Or maybe not even at all. That's a good plan," Mya said. They both ducked down and headed for the trail. Back at the house, Jason appeared in the living room holding Sky. Mike and Ava ran to her.

"Is she dead?" Ava asked.

"No, she's been drugged. Get grandma, please," Jason said. Ava ran to get Evelyn as Mike helped Jason lay Sky down on the couch. Michael walked over to her to see if he could help. He checked her for wounds and only found minor ones. Evelyn and Ava came running back into the room.

Evelyn kneeled down beside her. "We need a bowl of warm water, some rags, bandages, and some blood," Evelyn said. She turned around to see everyone still standing there. "Well…Hurry up!" Evelyn said again. Everyone started running around to grab everything while Evelyn stayed with Sky. They all came back and gave her everything they found.

"Where do we get the blood?" Mike asked. Evelyn pulled a small knife out of the cabinet beside her and made a small cut on her wrist.

"We get it from me," Evelyn said as she held her wrist against Sky's mouth. "Use the warm water and rag to wipe her face to get some of the dirt off of her," Evelyn said as she was still holding her wrist to Sky's mouth. Suddenly Sky woke up and grabbed her wrist and pushed it away.

"Where am I?" Sky asked in a shaky voice.

"Your home. Henry and Mya found you, and then I came to get you," Jason said as he took her hand. Mike just stood there looking at her, and Ava could see the sadness on his face. He felt as if he failed as her brother because he wasn't there to protect her. Ava grabbed his arm and hand, held herself close, and put her head on his shoulder. He put his other arm around her to hug her tight. This calmed him down a little. He let go of Ava slowly and leaned in to hug Sky.

"I'm so sorry, Sky. I should have been there to help you," Mike said.

"No! You did what you were told, and I thank you for that because they probably would have killed you," Sky said. As she let go of Mike, she turned to Evelyn, "I need to talk to you about something."

"What is it?" Evelyn asked.

Sky looked around at everyone. "Can we go talk somewhere else?" Sky asked.

Evelyn sat there for a minute and then stood up. "Yes. Follow me, and we will go to my room," Evelyn said in a confused voice. Sky stood up and went with Evelyn. As they walked into the room, Sky closed the door.

"Cast a spell to make the room private. We don't want anyone to listen in. Trust me," Sky said. Evelyn looked at her with a confused look but then walked to her closet and pulled out a candle.

"I used this to talk to Emma before the kids knew about magic," Evelyn said as she lit the candle.

"You may want to sit down for this," Sky said as she walked over to Evelyn's chair in the corner. Evelyn walked over to the bed and sat down.

"They didn't want me. They were going to trade me," Sky said.

"We figured so. We knew they would have wanted to finish the leader off," Evelyn said. Sky sat there quietly for a minute and shook her head no. Evelyn looked at her, confused.

"They wanted to trade me for Ava," Sky said.

"Ava? Why Ava? She said she thought they were after her, but I guess deep down, I didn't want it to be true," Evelyn said.

"This isn't even Iris's pack. There is a guy out there claiming to be Ava's father. Which is crazy, right? I mean, she isn't a vampire?" Sky queried. Evelyn got very quiet, stood up slowly, and started pacing. "Wait, you mean it's true? That vampire is her father? How? Does she know?" Sky asked.

"No… and she can't know. Not yet. We have to wait for Emma," Evelyn said.

"How does Ava not know she is a vampire?" Sky asked.

"Because she is half witch too, and that gives her more of a human side. Her vampire side might not even come to the surface. We have never even seen anyone born like her before. Her father was an injured warlock, and my sweet Emma saved him. She and Michel were separated at the time, and after she turned him, he met a group of vampires and joined them, who were Emma's friends. She ended up pregnant by him and then chose to get back with Michael before ever even finding out she was pregnant. After she found out, she told me and then told me who the father was. A half warlock, half vampire that she created," Evelyn said as she looked over at Sky.

Sky had no idea what to say at this point. "So who knows?" Sky asked.

"No one except Emma, me and you," Evelyn answered.

"Then how did he find out?" Sky asked.

"I'm not sure but I'm guessing magic," Evelyn said.

"We should head back out to the others before they suspect something," Sky said as she stood up and headed to the door.

"Don't tell Jason, please. We are going to tell them all, but Emma wants to be here when we tell them," Evelyn said. Sky turned and smiled in an agreeing way. She didn't like it, but she respected Evelyn, and for that, she would keep their secret.

As they walked back into the room, everyone was just standing around waiting for them. "What was so important you had to go to another room to talk?" Mike asked.

"It's not important. What are we doing now?" Sky asked. Jason walked over to peek out the window.

"Well, Henry and Mya are still out there. I couldn't bring you all back," Jason said.

"You left them alone? Well, forget the other vampires. They are going to kill each other," Sky said.

"Why do you say that?" Jason asked.

"They both have an opinion and don't like to listen to anyone else," Sky said as she laughed a little. Jason backed away from the window and looked over at everyone. "Someone is out there," Jason informed. Sky walked over to look. She turned and looked at Evelyn and then walked to the door. "Wait. I want to go out first. Stay inside," Jason said.

Just as he walked out the door, the vamp greeted him. "I'm Marko. Leader of," Marko said before being cut off.

"I know why you are here, and we are not giving you Iris back," Jason said.

"Who is Iris? I don't want her back. You can keep her. I want Ava," Marko said.

"Why do you want a witch that doesn't even have her magic yet?" Jason asked.

"You think this is about magic? Not even close. Bring her to me, and we will end all of this. I will even give you a day to spend with her to be nice. You have till tomorrow night," Marco said before turning around and starting to walk away. "By the way, if you want to see your girlfriend alive again, you will do what I say," Marco said.

"You mean this girlfriend?" Jason said sarcastically. Sky opened the door and walked outside. Jason could see the anger on his face as he turned and walked away.

Henry and Mya were just crossing the trail at that moment. Getting home would take longer, but they knew they could make it. They crossed the trail and came to a tightly wooded area where they could hide and take a break. They sat down but stayed quiet for a minute. "Why did you save me?" Mya asked.

"Do you really have to ask? We are on the same side, right?" Henry asked.

"You know what I mean, and before that, you held my hand," Mya said. Henry didn't say anything. "I see the way you have been looking at me, Henry. I just don't know why?" Mya asked. Henry leaned over quickly and kissed her. As he pulled away, Mya just sat there.

"I'm sorry," Henry said.

"Henry, kiss me again," Mya demanded as she smiled at him. Henry put his arms around her and guided her over, sat her in his lap, and kissed her again. Mya pulled away for a minute. "Are you sure about this?" Mya asked.

"Yes. I should have stayed with you before. I'm sorry I didn't realize sooner," Henry said. Mya leaned in and kissed him and she ran her fingers into the back of his hair and pulled his head back for a deeper kiss. Henry pulled away, pulled his shirt off, leaned back in, and started kissing her again. Things were getting heated, and things were about to change between them forever when they heard a noise. Mya jumped up, and Henry stood up and put her behind him.

"What was that?" Mya asked. Henry used his wolf eyes to look into the dark and saw a rabbit.

"It's just a rabbit," Henry said with relief, turning around to face Mya. He wrapped his arms around her to hold her and kissed her cheek. "Maybe we should keep moving," Henry said.

"I think you might be right. This probably isn't the best time," Mya said. They heard someone talking in the distance, so they ducked and looked around. The voices sounded like it was coming from the trail so they jumped up and ran toward the house. As they reached the top of the hill, they could see the house and the path they could take safely. "We need to run, as I can see them closing in," Mya said. They managed to run past all the vampires and in the front door. As they ran in and shut the door, everyone jumped up.

"You scared us," Evelyn said.

"Are you two ok?" Jason asked.

"Yes, we are good?" Henry said.

"Where is your shirt?" Ava asked. Henry looked down and realized he had left it in the woods.

"We must have left it in the woods," Henry said as he turned to Mya.

"If they find it, they will track us because it will have both our scents," Mya said in a worried voice.

"Both your scents?" Jason asked with a smile.

"Shut up, Jason," Henry said as he laughed a little. Ava looked at them both and turned to walk into the kitchen. Mike followed her.

"Are you ok?" Mike asked her. She turned and kissed him fast and hard. He picked her up, sat her on the counter, and pulled her close. Jason walked into the room and cleared his throat. Mike stepped back quickly, and both of them looked at Jason. "Don't hurt her, and keep her safe," Jason said, walking over to the table.

Mike got Ava down, and they walked over to the table with him and sat down. "What's wrong?" Ava asked.

"The vamp I talked to earlier wants you. I don't know why," Jason said.

"Over my dead body. I will rip his head clean off," Mike said.

"Good to know because we might have to," Jason said.

"I don't get why he would want to take me. I'm nothing special," Ava said.

"You are special to us, and that is all that matters," Mike said as he hugged her tight. Jason leaned in, put his arms on the table, and smiled at Mike. He talked to Mike in his head.

"That was a good answer," Jason said. Mike looked at him and smiled. Jason called Henry into the kitchen with his mind. Henry walked in to see Mike's arms around Ava. It bothered him a little but he couldn't say anything after what almost happened between him and Mya.

"Why did you call me?" Henry asked. Ava looked up to see Henry and pulled away from Mike a little but not entirely out of his arms.

"There was a vamp here earlier, and he wants Ava," Jason said.

"Did he say why?" Henry asked.

"Does it matter? He isn't getting her," Mike said.

"Calm down fangs. We are in agreement," Henry said sarcastically.

"You are one to talk. Yours are bigger than mine," Mike said.

"Are we still talking about fangs?" Henry asked with a smirk on his face.

"Alright, you two. We are here to protect Ava. Agreed?" Jason asked. Henry and Mike looked at each other and looked back at Jason.

"What's the plan?" Henry asked.

"We kill him," Jason answered. They all turned and walked to the living room.

"What's the plan?" Evelyn asked.

"Apparently, we are going to kill the vamp," Henry said.

"We need to do one more thing first," Jason said as he looked over at Branson.

"What's that?" Michael asked.

"We need to get mom," Jason informed.

CHAPTER 10

Everyone was still standing around comprehending what Jason said. "Branson, you know how these things work. I need you to talk us through it." Jason said.

"How do we find the door?" Michael asked.

"Well, the artifact and the door are one and the same. It will take Jason using his power to connect the two, and it should take you to her. But Jason, it's going to take a lot of power. A hunter uses amulets from other witches they kill and combines the power to create these prisons, so a counsel is needed for approval before it can be done. The hunter that took your mom must have killed a bunch to be able to create it on his own," Branson said.

"How do I connect the two?" Jason asked.

"Just sit and imagine a door, and you are holding the key, and you reach out to unlock the door to see your mom. You will begin to feel yourself moving through time. Once inside, you should be able to travel your mom and yourself back here," Branson answered.

"Should?" Michael said.

"Well, I have never been in one of the prisons. I have never put someone in one," Branson said.

Jason looked at Branson and Michael. "I'm going to give it a try," Jason said as he sat down on the floor and put the artifact in his lap while holding onto it. He closed his eyes and started to imagine a large door, and he was standing in front of it. He looked down and saw a key in his hand. As he put the key to the door, it opened, and Jason disappeared from the room, and the artifact was sitting on the floor.

"Is that supposed to happen?" Michael asked.

"I guess," Branson said as he looked at the floor where Jason was sitting before he vanished.

"So what now?" Michael said in a worried voice.

"Now we wait," Evelyn said.

Jason saw his mother standing in front of him. He was frozen in his steps as he had dreamed of the day he would see her since he found out she was alive. She walked over to him. "Jason, my son! I knew you would find me. You are so grown up," Emma said.

"Mom… This is real, right? Not just a dream?" Jason asked.

"No, I'm really here," Emma said with a laugh as she hugged him.

"Mom, there is so much to tell you, but we have to get back home. Take my hand, and don't let go," Jason said. Emma grabbed his hand with a smile, and Jason brought them both home. As they appeared in the living room everyone was so surprised. Evelyn ran to hug her, and Michael ran over and kissed her as soon as Evelyn let her go. Ava stood to the side, waiting to be seen. Emma turned to see Ava.

"Ava, my sweet daughter. I have missed you so much," Emma said as she held out her arms. Ava ran to her so fast, almost knocking her down. She was crying heavily as she was so happy to see her. "So, what did you need to tell me?" Emma asked as she turned to Jason.

"There are a bunch of vampires after Ava. The leader's name is Marco," Jason said.

"Marco," Emma said as she looked at Evelyn. "Looks like we need to have a talk, Ava. Michael I wish there was another way to tell you this as well. Let's all sit," Emma continued.

"You want us all to hear this?" Mike asked.

"Yes, as what is going on now will affect us all! Many years ago, when Jason was very little, Michael and I separated for a bit. I made some new witch and warlock friends. One of my friends got very sick and was dying, so I told him I could save him, but the only way to save him was to change him. He agreed as he knew what I was saying so I turned him into a vampire. We had never seen a warlock be turned into a vampire before so we weren't really sure what would happen. After being changed it turned out he still had his warlock powers as well. He started being mean to the others and couldn't stay with them, so he left to be with a vampire pack I had introduced him to. Now I wish I hadn't. They started killing witches and stealing their power. I told him I couldn't be around him anymore because I didn't agree with what he was doing, and he being a warlock vampire witch hunter, put me in prison and Ava, my sweet girl. He is also your father," Emma said it all in one go.

"What? Are you kidding me?" Ava said.

Emma looked over at Michael, who was furious, and she could see it on his face. "I'm so sorry. I didn't know I was pregnant till we got back together, and by then, I was scared to tell you. I planned to tell you after you bonded with her, but three months after she was born, I was put in that prison. Please forgive me," Emma said as she walked over to Michael. He stood there for a minute as he teared up. He grabbed her and hugged her. He wanted to be mad so bad but he was just so happy to have her home.

"So I'm a witch that's part vampire?" Ava asked. Emma and everyone turned to look at Ava.

"Yes," Emma said.

"How do I turn?" Ava asked.

"Turn?" Emma asked.

"If I'm part vampire, I should have fangs and be strong and fast, right?" Ava asked.

"I guess," Emma said.

"Maybe it has to be triggered. You know, like my wolf side," Henry said.

"That could be it," Evelyn said.

"Maybe I can teach you," Mike said. Ava turned around and smiled at Mike.

"I'm like you," Ava said with a big smile.

"Yes, you are," Mike said as he held out his hand. Ava took his hand, and they walked into the kitchen so he could try to teach her to turn.

They walked into the kitchen where they saw Sky sitting on the cabinet and Mya standing beside her. "I was wondering where your two went," Mike said.

"So you're one of us," Sky said as she got down off the cabinet.

"How did you?" Ava asked before being cut off.

"Vamp hearing, remember?" Sky said as she laughed. Ava smiled and sat down at the table.

"So, how does it work?" Ava asked.

"Well, for us, it's natural. We don't really have to try. It just happens," Mya said.

"Let's try something easy," Mike said as he walked over to the fridge. He grabbed a pack of meat. He opened it as he walked back over to the table. "Smell this and think of the juicy meat filled with blood," Mike said as he sat it in front of her on the table. Ava looked down at the steak, put her nose to it to smell it, looked back at Mike, and then jumped up to run to the trash and threw up.

"That smelled awful," Ava said.

"Well, that worked," Mya said sarcastically. "Well, when Jason kissed me, and I felt really heated, I started to turn," Sky said as she looked at Mike and Ava and shrugged her shoulders. Ava turned to Mike.

"It's worth a try," Ava said as she stood up and got in Mike's lap. She leaned in and kissed him very passionately. He grabbed her thighs, squeezed her, and pulled her closer. After a minute, Ava pulled away. "Well, I'm definitely heated, and I think we should go to my room, but I don't think this is working to turn me," Ava said as she looked Mike in the face, breathing heavily. She looked up behind Mike and saw Jason standing there and he didn't look happy. "Jason!" Ava said as she stood up quickly.

"Calm down. This was my idea. I turned when I kissed you outside that night, so I thought it might work," Sky said as she walked over to Jason.

"Did it work?" Jason asked.

"No," Ava said.

"Then why do you need to go to your room?" Jason asked.

"I would never do what she wants to do. I told her she was too young the last time I was with her," Mike said.

"Last time!" Jason said in a raised voice as he walked toward Mike. Sky put her hand against Jason and stopped him.

"She is growing up. You can't keep her innocent forever," Sky said.

"Keep who innocent?" Henry asked as he walked into the room.

"Me! Jason found out I almost had sex with Mike in my room, and he is mad about it. Like him and Sky don't feel like they want to," Ava said.

"What! When was Mike in your room?" Henry said as his eyes changed.

"Jason, look!" Ava said as she stepped in front of Mike and pointed at Henry. Jason turned to see Henry's eyes and grabbed him.

"Back out of the room, Henry, or I will send you to the barn to cool off," Jason said. Henry turned to walk away, followed by Jason.

"You can't be mad at her. You came home with Mya without a shirt on. You don't just lose your shirt. I'm guessing something happened between you two," Jason said as he stepped in front of Henry.

"I'm very attracted to her, but I'm not in love with her like I am with Ava," Henry said.

"Well, it looks like Ava has someone else in mind at the moment," Jason said. There was complete silence between the two for a minute. "Besides, we have more important things. Ava is a vampire witch. What are we even supposed to think and do?" Jason continued.

"Do you really think she is a vampire?" Henry asked.

"Mom seems to think so," Jason said.

"Doesn't seem to bother Ava any," Henry said.

"Yes, it does. She is just in shock. She will break down soon enough, and we will have to calm her down," Jason said.

The adults were still in the living room, talking about everything. As the boys return to the room, Evelyn has just finished filling Emma in on everything. "I am so proud of you, Jason. You have grown into a great young man. I just wish I could have seen it," Emma said as she walked over to hug him.

"So what do you think Marco wants?" Jason asked.

"He keeps trying to grab Ava. Is he planning on killing her?" Henry asked.

"I can't be sure, but he might be trying to bring her to his side. After all, the best way to hurt me is to turn her against me," Emma said.

"We won't let that happen," Evelyn said.

"He can't have her. I raised her, and she is my daughter!" Michael said in a raised voice. Ava heard him from the kitchen and came into the room, followed by Sky, Mya, and Mike.

"Isn't it my choice if I want to meet my father?" Ava asked.

"Ava baby, we don't know if he means you harm or not. We can't be sure of anything at the moment," Emma said as she walked over to her.

"Just stop! If you haven't noticed, Mom, I'm not a baby, and as for meaning me harm, I think he has had plenty of chances. If he has been the one coming into my room, why does he keep trying to grab me when he could just kill me? You are all just trying to keep me from knowing who I am and from meeting him!" Ava said in a raised voice.

"You could end up dead," Evelyn said.

"You could have told me… You knew this whole time… You kept it from me and knew what I am… Who my father is… Why should I listen to you?" Ava asked as she turned to Evelyn. Everyone stood there, not knowing what to say. Ava turned and walked to the stairs, then returned to the living room and stood there for a minute. "I'm done with all of you that has lied to me my whole life," Ava said as she headed up the stairs.

Mike was about to run after her, but Jason stopped him and turned to Henry. "Told you. Here is the breakdown. Let's go talk to her," Jason said as he walked toward the stairs. As the two of them went to the top of the stairs they heard loud noises coming from her room and ran to the door. They saw stuff lying all over the floor as they opened the door. She had grabbed trophies and pictures and many other things and smashed them.

"They are all lies. This isn't who I am meant to be." Ava said with anger.

"You are who you want to be," Jason said.

"What do you know? You're not even my brother." Ava said.

"I am... I am still your half-brother. We still have the same mom," Jason said as he walked over and hugged her. Henry slowly walked over to her.

"We still love you, Ava," Henry said, which made her mad again.

"You love me? Then why did you sleep with Mya? Don't act like nothing happened!" Ava said in a raised voice, making Mike come up the stairs.

"Nothing did happen. There was a noise, and we stopped," Henry said.

"So if it was quiet, you would have continued?" Ava asked in an angry voice.

"Probably best not to answer that," Jason said as he looked at both of them. Mike walked in and around Henry and over to Ava.

"Well, you almost slept with Mike," Henry said.

"Well, I guess it makes more sense to be with a vampire since I am one," Ava said as she leaned into Mike.

"HALF!" Henry yelled as he stepped toward them. Jason pushed him out the door into the hall and shut the door behind him.

"You have to calm down. You are only pushing her further from us. She will never calm down if you don't," Jason said.

"Fine. I'm going downstairs to see what the plan is," Henry said as he turned toward the stairs. Jason turned back toward Ava's door, not knowing what to say or do at this point, so he followed Henry down the stairs. As they got downstairs, everyone was quiet. Emma and Evelyn were sitting on the couch crying. Michael was standing in the middle of the living room, and Branson was gone.

"Where is Branson?" Jason asked.

"I think he went down into the basement to check on our guests," Michael said. Jason started toward the basement.

"Wait… Is she alright?" Emma asked.

"No, she is far from alright. She is mad, sad, and feeling betrayed." Jason said. Emma looked down at the floor and started crying all over again.

"How did you handle it so well when we told you?" Evelyn asked.

"I felt the same way she did. I just got over it. She will too, but in her own time and way," Jason said as he turned to walk away. He walked down the stairs to the basement and found Branson standing there.

"Why does he want her? Look, we know what she is, but we don't know why he wants her," Branson said, looking at the vampires.

"No answers, huh?" Jason asked. Branson turned around to see Jason standing on the stairs, leaning against the wall with his arms crossed.

"I didn't hear you come down," Branson said as he approached Jason.

"Well, then it's a good thing I wasn't a bad guy," Jason said with a smile. Branson laughed and sat down on the stairs. "I never thanked you for all your help. I want you to know you don't have to stay. I saved you, and you helped save my mom. We are even," Jason said as he held out his hand to Branson.

"I know I don't have to stay, but I know right from wrong, and you guys don't deserve what's happening. I'm staying till everything is over or until I die. Whichever comes first," Branson said with a laugh as he shook Jason's hand. Jason laughed as well.

"Emma is back?" The tall vampire said.

"Maybe… What if she is? What are you going to do about it?" Jason asked. The vampire got very quiet and turned away from Jason.

"Apparently nothing," Branson said with a laugh. Jason turned and went back upstairs, followed by Branson.

Ava and Mike were still up in her room and he was trying to clean up her room. "I don't know what I am. I'm a vampire witch, and I can't use either one. I'm a nothing," Ava said as she sat on her bed.

"You're not nothing, Ava. You're the girl that made me smile. When I first met you, I didn't want to like you. I wanted to walk into the party with you as my date to make Jason mad. He was dating my sister, so I was going to date his. When I saw you that night, you were so beautiful; your smile made me forget everything. I couldn't believe you were my date. As the night went on, we laughed so much and had so much fun that I couldn't help but like you. That's why I asked you to take a walk with me. I was going to tell you what I was and that I wanted to be with you and only you. Then we found that hurt girl and you freaked out. I knew it wasn't the time," Mike said as he sat down beside her. He put his arm around her and took her hand. She looked at him and smiled.

"If I asked you to do something, would you do it?" Ava asked.

"Yes?" Mike said in a worried voice.

"I want you to go find my father. I want him to know I want to meet him. I can't do it because they won't let me out of here. You could jump out the window and return before they knew you were gone," Ava said.

"Ava, anything but that. He will kill me. How do I tell a guy who murders people for fun," Mike said before being cut off.

"He isn't a murderer. No one has proof of that," Ava said in a sad voice. Mike sat there for a minute. He wanted to make her happy, but he didn't want to die either.

"Take off your shirt," Mike said as he stood up in front of her.

"What?" Ava asked in a confused voice.

"Your father knows your scent. He will smell the shirt, and the one on you now will have your strongest scent. He will smell me coming, and then when I tell him you want to see him, he will know I'm telling the truth, and maybe I will live," Mike said as he held out his hand.

Ava slowly took her shirt off and handed it to Mike. He stood there looking at her for a second. She stood up and got really close to him. "Maybe you should stay for a minute," Ava said, and she kissed him. He kissed her back but then grabbed a shirt from the chair beside her bed and handed it to her. "Why do you fight it? I know you want to," Ava protested.

"Because I don't want it to be like this. You're doing this because you're stressed out, and I don't want you to regret it later. Our first time should be in calmness and when we least expect it," Mike said as he put his hand on her face and kissed her. Ava smiled because it was sweet.

"Fine, we will wait," Ava said.

Mike turned to the window and then turned back. "Wish me luck," Mike said before jumping out.

Ava walked downstairs quietly and saw everyone sitting in the living room. She was going to the basement for some answers. As she walked down, one of the vampires spoke, "I can smell you, princess. Thought you weren't allowed down here," The tall one said as she got to the bottom of the stairs.

"I'm not, so keep it down, will you?" Ava asked.

"Sure thing, princess," The tall one said.

"What is your name?" Ava asked.

"John, I'm your dad's right-hand man," John said.

"What does my father want with me?" Ava asked.

"To get to know you, of course," John said.

"That's it?" Ava asked another question.

"Well he would like for you to come with us. He didn't even know you existed, so he feels cheated on helping raise you," John said with a smile.

"So he isn't here to hurt anyone?" Ava asked.

"If you were with him, he would leave everyone alone," John said with a big smile. Ava saw the smaller vampire looking at the taller one with an aggravated face.

"And who are you?" Ava asked.

"That's my little brother, Tim," John said.

"You don't talk, Tim?" Ava asked. He turned away from her.

"If you help me out of here, I will take you to him," John said.

"I don't know if that's a good idea," Ava said.

"Sure it is! Look, just come closer, and I will tell you where he is," John said. Ava slowly started walking over to him, and Tim grabbed John and pushed him against the wall.

"LEAVE HER ALONE!" Tim yelled which caught the attention of everyone upstairs. Jason and Henry came running downstairs.

"Ava… What are you doing down here?" Jason asked.

"I wanted to know more about my father, and John said…" Ava said before being cut off.

"Who is John?" Jason asked.

"That is John, and that is Tim." Ava pointed at each one.

"Did they talk to you?" Jason asked.

"Yes… I think John was going to hurt me, though, because he told me if I came closer, he would tell me where my father was, and Tim attacked him. I think he was trying to save me," Ava said.

"You tried to hurt her?" Henry asked as he ran over, grabbed John, and shoved him to the ground. He started punching and kicking him. Jason pulled him off and John stood up laughing.

"Well, that was fun," John said.

"Do I need to let him go at it again?" Jason asked.

"Please do," Henry said.

"You… come with us," Jason said as he pointed at Tim.

"Don't you tell them anything!" John said to Tim in a raised voice as they all walked up the stairs and left him in the basement alone.

They walked into the living room with Tim, and everyone else was just looking at him. "This is Tim. He stopped his brother from hurting me," Ava said.

"Yea… Thanks for that! Now tell us why," Henry said. Tim stood there, quiet.

"Unless you want to go back down there with your brother," Jason continued. Tim looked at Ava. She walked over to him and took his hand.

"You are safe. Please tell us why you saved me," Ava said. Tim looked around the room for a minute.

"Ava, you're my sister. I would have never hurt you earlier. I just needed some of your blood to try and escape," Tim said. Ava stepped back.

"I'm your what?" Ava asked.

"How?" Jason asked.

"So John is my brother too?" Ava asked.

"NO! Our dad got with his mom. He's my stepbrother and a jerk," Tim said.

Ava looked at Tim and smiled. She was so excited. "Now I have two brothers," Ava said.

"I know I don't know her too well, but Ava is my sister, and I had to protect her. Our dad doesn't want to hurt you, but my stepbrother does," Tim said.

"Why does he want to hurt Ava?" Michael asked.

"Really, it's my stepmom. She is pregnant and is having a girl and was so excited that she was giving him his first girl," Tim said.

"How did Marco even find out about Ava?" Emma asked.

"Well, he got a call about the missing artifact that was the key to your prison, so he came to see if you managed to get Emma out. When he got close, he could smell Ava, and he knew she was his. Now he wants her, and my stepmom wants her dead from jealousy," Tim said.

"Makes sense. She is his first-born daughter," Emma said.

"How old are you?" Ava asked.

"About to be fifteen," Tim said.

"Your dad must have moved on quickly since Ava also turned fifteen," Evelyn said.

"That's not important. We have to figure out what's going on and how to save my sister. I would like to be able to get to know her, which won't be possible if she is dead," Tim said as he turned to Ava.

"Take Tim to the kitchen while we talk about some things," Emma said as she put her hand on Ava's shoulder. As Ava and Tim got to the kitchen, she sat down in a chair, and Tim sat beside her.

"So you're my half-brother, and our father wants me to come with you?" Ava asked.

"Yes, but…" Tim said and then stopped.

"But what?" Ava asked.

"You should stay here. It's not safe with him. Ava, your family here loves you and protects you. It's different out there," Tim said as he turned and looked at her.

"Then why do you stay?" Ava asked.

"Because it's all I have ever known. I have nowhere else to go. I don't have a safe place," Tim said as he looked down at the table.

"I want to meet him, though. I want to see where I come from," Ava said.

"He is going to be a disappointment. I'm sorry, but it's true. He has killed lots of witches to get the magic he needed to do what he did to your mom," Tim said. Ava looked away. She hated hearing her real father was a bad guy.

"But he has stopped now, right?" Ava asked.

"I won't lie to you, Ava. It's been a while since he has killed, but I don't think he has stopped. He just hasn't had a reason to," Tim said. After a long pause, Tim turned to Ava. "If I had somewhere else to go, I wouldn't be there, and I don't want you to go through what I have. He has made me kill, and I know he will again, and I don't want him to do the same to you," Tim said in a sad voice.

"I won't kill anyone," Ava said.

"You will if he tells you to, or you die. I would only kill willingly for one reason, and that's you, Ava. I will protect you while I'm around. That's what brothers do," Tim said as he hugged her.

Everyone else was still in the living room arguing about what to do with Tim. "So we are just going to let this vampire we don't know run through the house with Ava?" Henry said.

"He's her brother, and I don't think he will hurt her," Sky said.

"Think? Well, sorry, Sky, but *think* isn't good enough for me," Henry said.

"We could send him back with a message saying to leave and that he isn't getting Ava," Michael said.

"Then he is going to have another fighter on his side. Think about it. He said he wanted to get to know Ava. If he can't do that here, he will help take her," Evelyn said.

"This is madness. Let's just go kill them all already," Mya said.

"I like her idea. Starting with Tim," Henry said as he started to walk to the kitchen.

"Look, everyone, just calm down. This isn't going to help Ava. It's just going to start more trouble if we kill them," Emma said.

"Well, if we can't kill them or send them back, then what do we do with them?" Michael said. Everyone stood there quietly.

"Do you want to chime in here?" Michael said as he turned to Branson.

"Oh no… this is a family matter. I'm just here for the fight," Branson said. Suddenly, the front door opened, and Rick walked in with the other vampires.

"What is going on?" Rick asked as he looked around at everyone. You could see everyone was on edge.

"Go to the kitchen, and Ava will fill you in, and don't hurt the vampire," Jason said as Rick walked by. As he walked into the kitchen, he saw Tim sitting there.

"Why are you in here?" Rick asked protectively as he walked closer.

"This is my half-brother," Ava said as she got between them. Rick looked at her, confused. "Oh right, you have missed all the fun stuff. Marco, the leader of the pack outside, is my real dad, and this is his son. He wants to get to know me," Ava continued.

"Marco? That's who is leading that pack?" Rick asked.

"Yes?" Ava said in a confused voice.

"I was part of his pack but left shortly after because he started killing witches," Rick said.

"Yea, well, he took their magic to put Emma in prison," Tim said.

"He is the one that put your mom in the prison?" Rick asked as he turned to Ava. She looked away. She wasn't sure what to say at that point.

"We need you guys back in here for a minute," Jason called from the living room. As they all walked into the room everyone was looking at Tim. "We need to ensure you're not going to hurt Ava," Jason said.

"He had his chance in the kitchen. We were in there all alone," Ava said as she looked at Jason.

"She has a point," Branson added.

"Now you want to talk," Michael said as he looked over at Branson. He just smiled at Michael and stepped back.

"I will gladly fight for her," Tim said.

"Against your own father?" Henry asked.

"He hasn't been my father for a long time," Tim said.

"He should stay with us after this," Ava said. Everyone looked at her. "He doesn't like it with Marco. He said that he just stays there because he doesn't have anywhere to go. Well, we could let him stay here," Ava said as she smiled at everyone.

"Well, let's try to make it through the night first," Michael said.

CHAPTER 11

The sun was starting to rise, and they hadn't attacked. Everyone was starting to wonder what the plan was. They could hear them in the distance, but that was just it. They were staying far away. "What could they be waiting for?" Jason thought to himself.

"This is just taking forever. Why don't we just run over there and kill them, and where is Iris?" Rick asked.

"She has been in my room sleeping all night," Evelyn answered.

"We will not be the first to draw blood," Jason said. Rick didn't like Jason's words, so he walked over to Emma.

"I'm really glad you are here. I remember you saved my life, and I would like to return the favor. If you will let me I will take a group and end this," Rick offered.

"What happens if he kills you all? Then what? How will you return the favor, then… I trust my son. He has led them all this far, and I believe he can do it again. Marco has magic and could kill you all so easily, but with Jason on your side, he can block his magic. He just needs to learn how. Find me something to enchant. It can be anything as long as there is one for each of you," Emma said as she looked at Rick excitedly as the idea finally hit her. Rick started looking around the whole house as he wanted to help Emma. He even got the other vamps to help. "I have an idea," Emma continued as she walked out into the middle of the room. Everyone turned to look at her. "A protection charm… It will keep everyone safe during a fight," Emma said.

"Not if Marco figures it out and takes it away," Evelyn added.

"By the time he realizes what's going on, it will be too late. We move fast and hard," Emma said as she looked around the room.

"I think it's worth a shot. Mom has done these things before, and I trust her. That's why I wanted her here for this," Jason said as he looked around the room and then turned to Emma.

"So what are you going to enchant?" Ava asked.

"These!!" Rick said as he came running into the room and threw them all on the table.

"Beans? Really? You're joking, right?" Henry said. Emma turned to look at Rick.

"It was all I could find," Rick said as he gave Emma a sorry look.

"This is perfect. He will never see them, and it will take forever for him to find out what is going on. We can enchant these, and then everyone can put them in their pocket, which will be hard to find," Emma said as she picked up all the beans.

"Mom, I know you want to protect everyone, but we need to ensure this will work. We need a backup plan as well," Jason said. Emma started her spell to enchant the beans.

"What do you have in mind?" Henry asked Jason.

"We don't need one," Ava replied.

"What makes you say that?" Henry was confused. Ava looked at the ground. She was scared to tell them what she did. "Ava, what's going on?" Henry asked another question.

"I just have my own plan," Ava said.

"I'm done. Everyone needs to take a bean. Just put it in your pocket if you have one or find another place, like in your shoe." Emma informed. She handed them out to the vampires first, then gave one to Jason, Henry, and Ava. Ava looked at hers for a minute. "Just put it in your pocket. It will make me feel better," Emma said. Ava took the bean and put it in her pocket. "We still have two left. Who hasn't got a bean?" Emma asked.

"Who didn't get a bean?" Jason asked the same question.

"One should be Iris's," Evelyn said.

"But what about the last one... Is someone missing?" Jason queried.

Ava knew it was time to speak up. "It belongs to Mike... I sent him to see my father," Ava said.

"You did what?" Jason asked as he turned to her.

"Why did you send him alone?" Sky asked as she walked over to her.

"I want to meet my father. I want to know why he did what he did. He has answers to a bunch of questions, and he is going to tell me," Ava answered.

"IT DOESN'T MATTER AVA… YOU DON'T JUST!" Jason yelled before Sky put up her hand to stop him.

"Leave her be. I understand what she is going through. I would want answers, too. She is doing what any of us would have done," Sky said.

"Let's just hope he comes back alive," Mya said. Everyone turned to look at her.

"Yea, let's hope," Henry said sarcastically.

Ava turned and slapped him. "Don't you dare Henry… You are with Mya and don't you lie to me about it. I'm not the only one that moved on. You just don't like that it's with a vampire. Well, guess what, Henry? I am a vampire. I don't need protection. I can take care of myself," Ava said.

"Really, Ava, then why haven't you turned yet?" Henry asked.

Ava was about to slap him again, and Jason grabbed her and pulled her back. "Calm down, Ava. Just step back and breathe," Jason said as Michael walked over to grab her. Jason let her go and walked back over to Henry. "Why did you have to get her started,

Henry?" Jason asked in an aggravated voice. Henry just shrugged his shoulders. He didn't mean to and didn't know what to say. At that moment, they heard a loud thump outside on the porch.

"What was that?" Ava asked.

"I'm not sure," Jason said as he walked to the door. He opened it and saw Mike lying on the porch covered in blood.

"MIKE!" Ava yelled as she ran outside to him. She started crying heavily.

"What happened to him?" Sky asked as she ran outside.

"I'm not sure. Let's get him inside," Jason said. Sky helped him pick Mike up and carry him to the couch. Ava followed closely.

The other vampires looked very upset as soon as they set him down. "Rick, I need all the vampires outside. They were close. He did not make it to the porch alone," Jason said as he looked at him.

Rick looked at the others and then took off out the door. "Surround the house and kill anything that moves," Rick ordered. Back in the house, Ava refused to leave Mike's side. She sat on the floor and held his hand.

"What are we going to do now? Apparently, Marco doesn't want to play nice," Henry said.

"Why would he attack Mike if he wanted Ava to go with him? He should know that it would make her mad," Jason said.

"I'm not sure, but I don't think we can walk up and ask him," Henry said sarcastically.

"This is no time for jokes, Henry," Jason said.

"Who's joking?" Henry asked. Mike started to wake up slowly.

"Mike! Mike, it's me, Ava," Ava said. Mike opened his eyes a little and looked at her.

"So your dad… not such a bad man. Your stepmom, on the other hand, is another story," Mike said as he gripped Ava's hand. Jason walked over to Mike.

"What did he say?" Jason asked.

"Well, he wants to meet Ava. He isn't here to hurt her or anyone, but he will if he has to so he can meet her. We actually sat down to have a good talk. His wife watched us like a hawk, and then when I left, she had vampires jump me. Marco thinks he's running the show, but it's really her," Mike said as he sat up. "He wants me to bring Ava to him, but I won't do it because I think she will kill Ava," Mike said.

"Here… Drink," Ava said as she held out her arm. Mike looked at her for a minute. "Wouldn't be a bad idea to be full strength. If she wants Ava that bad, she isn't going to let these walls and vampires stop her," Jason said as he walked away. He knew what needed to be done but didn't want to watch his sister get bitten. Mike bit into Ava's arm slowly. He felt bad for what he had to do.

Rick walked back inside and over to Jason. "They must have dropped him in a hurry because they are gone," Rick informed.

"Would he be mad if he knew what she was doing?" Jason asked as he turned to Tim.

"He would. But how are you going to tell him?" Tim asked.

"I need to look into your memories. I need you to think about your dad's tent out there. I need to see inside it: tables, chairs, bed, anything in there," Jason said as he put one hand on each side of Tim's head.

"Can you do that?" Tim asked.

"We are about to find out," Jason said.

"What are you doing?" Henry asked.

"Remember my magic trick?" Jason asked as he looked over at Henry and then looked back. Jason closed his eyes and felt his power flow through his hands and connect at Tim's head. At first, it was just flashes. "Tim, it's fine. Don't fight it," Jason said as he dug deeper. Tim cleared his mind and thought of nothing but standing in the middle of his dad's tent. Jason finally got a clear view as if he was standing right there. He saw a table by the bed and knew what to do. He moved his hands slowly from Tim's head. "Are you ok?" Jason asked.

"Yes… Did you see it?" Tim asked.

"Yes. Someone get me some paper and a pen," Jason said as he looked around the room. Emma ran to him with a pen and paper when suddenly Evelyn's phone rang.

"It's Sandy," Evelyn said.

Emma put her hand out to get the phone, excited to talk to her best friend again. "Hello, Sandy," Emma said. At first there was silence and then crying. Sandy knew her best friend's voice so well.

"How is this possible? They got you out?" Sandy asked.

"Jason did. He's very special," Emma said as she looked at Jason.

"I'm outside the ring of vampires with the pack. We can't get through without being seen," Sandy said.

Emma turned to Jason. "I heard her. Tell her to wait for her chance because I will fix it," Jason said.

He started writing the note: Marco, I know we did not get off to a good start, but in our defense, you didn't exactly knock on the door, and we didn't know who you were. Ava has no problem meeting you; believe it or not, we don't want to fight, and I have heard from your son Tim that you don't either. However, there is a problem. Your wife does. When you sent Mike on his way earlier she had him jumped and beaten to send a message. Well, here is yours. She wants Ava dead. Come to the door, and we will let you meet Ava. Jason then put the note in his hand and sent it to the table beside Marco's bed.

"When he shows up, everyone, be nice. We need him to want to help us because, besides me, he's the only other powerful one like me," Jason said.

"Yeah, with stolen magic," Henry said.

"Doesn't matter how he got it at the moment. Just that he can help and from inside the circle at that," Jason said.

They had been waiting all day for Marco to come. It was starting to get dark again, and suddenly, there was a knock at the door. Jason walked over, peeked out, and saw a man standing there. He opened the door slowly. "Are you alone, Marco?" Jason asked.

"Yes," Marco answered.

Jason opened the door wider as a gesture to come in. Marco walked in slowly, and standing in the middle of the room were Ava and Mike; he had his arms around her in a protective way. Marco walked over to her slowly. "I'm assuming you know who I am by now?" Marco asked.

"I do. You're my father," Ava answered. Marco smiled and held out his hand to shake hers. Ava looked at Jason, who was standing behind Marco. He gave her a nod that it was fine, and she took Marco's hand. "I have questions for you," Ava said as she released his hand. Marco stayed quiet. "Why did you put my mom away?" Ava asked.

"I was upset. I know now it was wrong and I wanted to release her but didn't have the power to do it," Marco said.

"It was wrong? IT WAS WRONG! You took my mom away from us. What would you have done if she were still pregnant with me? She is lucky she had me before," Ava said.

"I know, and if I could go back," Marco said before being cut off.

"You would what? Make things right? Well, you can do it now and stop attacking my family," Ava said.

"I haven't attacked anyone," Marco said with a confused look.

"What about Sky and Mike? You kidnapped Sky and had Mike beaten," Ava said.

"It wasn't me. Honestly, I didn't know they were going to do all those things. I was told Sky was tied up. Yes! But I didn't order it," Marco said.

"They drugged her, too," Ava said.

Marco looked sad at Sky. "I am so sorry that happened to you. If I would have known," Marco said as he looked away.

"Like Ava said, you can make it right now. We have friends that need through the circle. Call your men away so they can move through without being seen. As for your wife, I know she is pregnant, but they will kill her if she tries to attack them," Jason said. Marco looked at Ava with sadness in his eyes. Then he looked at Jason.

"I will call them away. I will also handle my wife. Tim also looks happy, but where is my stepson?" Marco asked.

"The basement. He keeps trying to kill Ava," Tim said.

"Do you mind if I go down there?" Marco asked as he turned to Jason. Jason turned toward the door and opened it to let Marco down the stairs.

As he reached the bottom, John turned to see his father standing there. "Dad!!! What are you doing here? They won't let me go. Get me out of here," John said. Marco just stood there looking at him for a minute.

"Did you try to kill my daughter?" Marco asked. John just stood there. He was scared to speak.

"Well, are you going to answer him?" Jason asked as he leaned up against the wall.

"Dad, I wouldn't have killed her. I just wanted a hostage to get out of here. She's my sister," John said.

"No, she's my sister, and I wouldn't have put her in harm's way like that," Tim said as he walked downstairs.

"You are just a little pet, aren't you? You don't ever do anything wrong. The perfect son. Good thing we are not actually related, or I might have to be like that too. The little princess would have got what she deserved," John said. Marco got very upset and walked over to John, who started groveling immediately. "Dad, I'm sorry. I didn't mean it," John said as Marco grabbed him by the neck and squeezed till his neck broke. Then he set the body on fire with a wave of his hand, and they watched him burn as Marco contained the fire with his power.

"His mother won't be happy, but he was a bad seed to begin with," Marco said as he walked back up the stairs. Tim walked over to Ava.

"Don't go in the basement," Tim said as he hugged her.

"What about John?" Evelyn asked.

"Oh, Marco took care of it," Jason said with a smile.

"He won't be after Ava anymore, but I'm sorry about the mess in the basement. I'm sorry for many things and will start trying to make them right," Marco said as he walked over and opened the front door. He turned back and looked at Jason. "Give me ten minutes, and my people will be gone. Then your friends can come through," Marco said. As he closed the door, Jason locked it.

"So he's met Ava and killed his stepson. He apologized to everyone and said he would let our friends come through. Does anyone else feel like this is too easy?" Henry asked.

"I have to agree with Henry on this one," Mya said as she stepped forward. Jason just looked around the room.

"You know him better than any of us. Do you think he is telling the truth?" Jason asked as he walked up to Emma.

"I think it's possible. The old him, I believe, would have tried to kill us all. I guess there is a chance he has changed," Emma said.

Jason turned to Tim. "Why did he send you to the house?" Jason asked.

"He didn't… When they came out yelling, John told us we needed to make the other vampires pay. I didn't want to do anything, but he was Dad's second in command, and I had to listen to him," Tim said.

"I am trusting you to help with my sister and not get her killed or kidnapped," Jason said as he turned to walk away. Tim grabbed Jason's arm and stopped him, and Jason turned to look at him. "She's my sister too, remember," Tim said as he looked Jason in the eyes and let go.

"It's been 10 minutes, Jason," Ava said as she grabbed his hand and looked worried.

"It's time," Emma said as she grabbed her phone, dialed Sandy's number, and sat the phone down on the table on speaker.

"Did you guys come up with a plan yet?" Sandy asked.

"Marco was just here. He said he would call the vampires away so that you can get through with the pack. Do you see them?" Emma asked.

"I see a few, but some of them have walked away," Sandy answered.

"Can you get through without being seen?" Jason asked.

"I think we can. If something happens, I will give you a call." Sandy said.

"As soon as Sandy arrives with the wolf pack, we will tell them to leave or fight. I am tired of hiding inside. We know what we can do, and if I can learn more of my power, I could defend us better," Jason said.

"Or you could end up weak and get killed," Sky said as she walked over to him.

"How should he learn if he can't try new things? We have to trust him. He is the strongest one here," Henry said.

"You're right, but the problem is we don't know how his powers work," Michael said.

"I do! I guess that's one of the good things about being a hunter. You see your fair share of magic after being around so many witches and warlocks. I can tell you of a few things, but of course, I can't show you." Branson said as he walked over to Jason.

"Let's go in here and talk," Jason said as he pointed to the kitchen.

They walked over to the table and sat down. "First off, you need to know that your power comes from inside. So your energy is your power. If you don't have energy, you have no power, so it's very important to pay attention to how tired you feel," Branson said.

"I can do that," Jason said.

"You need to learn how to control others. You have to visualize them doing what you want them to do," Branson said.

"As in, I want a drink and I make Henry come in here and do it," Jason said.

"Technically, yes but I would start by someone in the same room and making them pick up a pencil or something small. Then you can move on to other rooms and possibly other places. Not sure just how strong you are yet. Here, you can practice on me," Branson said as he stood up from his chair. Jason slowly stood up.

"What if I accidentally hurt you?" Jason asked.

"Wouldn't be the first time," Branson said with a laugh as he set a plate, apple, and a napkin on the table.

"Make me pick something up," Branson said as he looked at Jason. Jason tried to picture Branson picking up the apple, but he didn't do it.

"How is this going to help anyway?" Jason asked.

"If you could control people, you could make them leave. They wouldn't be able to harm anyone," Branson answered.

"That is a lot of vampires to control," Jason said in an aggravated voice.

"You're right, but you are not controlling them all. I don't even think you could. Besides this only works to stop them from harm at the moment. Once you lose focus, they are back in control," Branson said.

"Okay, I will try again," Jason said.

"Focus on me. Picture my hand moving and doing what you want it to," Branson said. Jason looked down at Branson's hand and pictured it moving over to the apple and picking it up. Slowly, his hand started to move, and he grabbed the apple. Jason then had him set it on the plate. "Good. Now, what do you want me to do?" Branson asked. Jason was just shocked he did it and didn't know what to say.

"I did it. We should try cutting the apple," Jason said excitedly.

"Hold on a second. I'm not trying to lose a finger," Branson laughed.

Back in the living room the others were waiting on Sandy. Emma was watching out a small hole in the curtain. Henry was sitting there in a blank stare. "What's wrong?" Mya asked as she sat down beside Henry.

"I have never met the pack before. Honestly, I think I'm still getting used to the idea of being a wolf," Henry said as he looked over at her.

"Are you worried they won't approve of you?" Mya asked.

"I'm not sure; I just feel I'm not like them. I feel like I don't belong," Henry answered.

"I can't say you belong with them because I don't know them, but I can say you belong here, and we can't do this without you," Mya said with a smile. Suddenly, everyone heard a loud crash in the kitchen. Henry jumped up and ran in to check on them. Jason is standing there laughing hysterically, and Branson is covered in fresh farm raw eggs that were once on top of the fridge. The fridge was wide open and a shelf was on the floor with some food.

"What happened?" Henry asked.

Branson looks over at Henry. "Jason was having me get something out of the fridge and didn't pay attention to how he placed my arm, and I ended up leaning on the shelf, and well, the rest is all over me and the floor," Branson said. Henry started laughing as well.

"What happened to my kitchen?" Evelyn asked as she walked in.

"Well," Jason said before she cut him off.

"Never mind. I don't care what happened, but you two better clean it up," Evelyn said as she looked at Jason and Branson before walking back to the living room.

Marco was having some issues of his own. He had learned that some of his people were against him, and he needed to get them back or force them to leave. To do either, he needs to prove a statement. He called for his wife.

"You called for me?" Misty said as she walked in.

"I just visited my daughter. She is a very sweet girl. I also saw your son," Marco said as he looked up at her.

"John? Is he over there? I have been wondering where he went," Misty said as she looked away from him.

"Yes, he is over there. We had a nice chat. Tim too; Learned a few things about my pack, about you as well," Marco said as he walked over to her.

"What kind of things? Are they keeping him over there? Is he ok?" Misty asked.

"He was," Marco replied.

"Why do you say was? As past tense not anymore?" Misty asked.

"You sent him to kill my daughter?" Marco asked as he grabbed her arm. The fear on her face was noticeable. She was not sure what he would do at this point.

"I'm sorry. I just didn't want our daughter to lose you," Misty murmured.

"You mean you wanted me to yourself and didn't want anyone else to get any of my attention," Marco said as he released her arm and gave it a shove away.

"I'm pregnant with our daughter. I couldn't just let you ignore us," Misty protested.

"I wouldn't have. I just wanted to meet my daughter, that I never knew existed. Maybe I would have if I wasn't so wrapped up in my own life," Marco said as he turned away from her.

"Let's just leave. We can go somewhere nice and have our little girl. We don't need to add more drama to what is already here. We can get John and Tim and just go," Misty tried to sort things out as soon as possible.

Marco turned and looked at her. "I'm afraid it's too late for that. You see, you sent your son to kill my daughter, and I did what I had to so I could protect her," Marco said. Misty just looked at him with a confused look. "Your son is dead," Marco said.

"YOU KILLED HIM!" Misty yelled.

"YES, I DID, AND IT WOULD NEVER HAVE HAPPENED IF YOU WOULDN'T HAVE SENT HIM TO KILL AVA!" Marco yelled back.

"As soon as you have my daughter, I want you gone, but she is staying with me. I'm not going to let you raise our daughter the way you raised Tim," Marco said.

"Don't act so innocent, Marco. You have killed plenty. Your hands are just as stained as mine," Misty said as she wiped the tears from her eyes.

"Yes, they are, but I'm still washing mine clean. Yours are getting darker," Marco said as he looked over at her. Misty turned around and walked out of the tent. Marco followed her out into the crowded area. "John will not be with us anymore," Marco announced to everyone. They all looked around, confused. "TELL THEM WHY; GO AHEAD; YOU DIDN'T HAVE A PROBLEM DOING IT OR TELLING ME!" Misty yelled from across the crowd.

Marco stood there looking at her for a minute. "HE KILLED HIM!" Misty yelled.

"YOU'RE RIGHT, AND IF YOU WEREN'T PREGNANT WITH OUR DAUGHTER, I WOULD KILL YOU TOO! YOU SENT HIM TO KILL MY DAUGHTER, AND… THAT I CAN'T FORGIVE!" Marco yelled out. "Misty is banished as soon as the baby is born, and anyone who wants to join her is free to leave. I will not tolerate betrayal or disobedience," Marco said as he turned and walked back to his tent. He was followed by one of his vampires.

"Sir, I heard others talking earlier about Ava and that she was going to be taken care of. I tried to find you. Is she ok?" The vampire said.

"She is fine, Jessy. You will get to meet her soon as well. Have I told you that you are both the same age?" Marco asked as he turned around and sat down in a chair.

"No sir, you haven't, but I would love to meet her," Jessy said as he smiled.

"I want you to deliver a message for me. Tell them Marco sent you; you are the new right hand." Marco said. Jessy gave him a nod.

Back at the house, everyone was trying to figure out what they would do if Marco couldn't handle his wife. Ava and Mike were in her room, Jason and Henry were in his room, and Sky and Mya were downstairs in the kitchen with a few of the vampires while everyone else was in the living room. There was so much silence with the adults as they all sat lost in their thoughts. "Do we honestly just let the kids handle this? I'm sorry; I just can't handle the silence anymore. They are just kids. We should be doing something," Sandy said as she stood up.

"What do you think we should do? The better question is, what can we do? Jason is stronger than all of us and has proved it many times already. We have to let him be the leader here. He has a great idea. Marco will help us. We won't have to fight," Evelyn said.

Sandy sat back down slowly. "I hope you're right," Sandy said as she rested her head in her hands. Everyone was worried about the kids. They just didn't want to admit it.

In the kitchen, Sky was putting a plan together and instructing her pack. "If they come in, we have to protect Ava. We know that's who they want," Sky said as she looked at everyone.

"Do you think Marco won't be able to control them?" Mya asked.

Sky shook her head and looked at the floor and back at Mya. "Honestly, I don't know. We all know how a vampire can get. We might be the only ones besides Jason that can stop them," Sky answered.

"If that's true, then we will be in big trouble. There are way too many people here to protect. How will we be able to fight and keep an eye on everyone?" Rick asked.

"He's right, Sky. We need to send people away." Mya said.

"Jason is the one to make that decision," Sky said as she looked around at everyone. Jason and Henry were waiting to hear from Marco.

"What do we do if this doesn't work out?" Henry questioned.

"It will. I have to trust Marco. He didn't hurt anyone and killed John for trying to hurt Ava. Why would he do that if he wanted to hurt us?" Jason said as he looked at Henry. As they sat there, they heard a knock at the door. They both ran downstairs as Evelyn was about to open the door.

"Stop! Don't open it," Jason said as he came down the stairs. He ran up beside her. "Step back, Grandma. I don't want you to get hurt." Jason said as he squeezed between her and the door. She stepped back to let him open the door. He looked out and saw Jessy standing there. "Who are you?" Jason asked.

"My name is Jessy. I have been appointed Marco's new right hand. He asked me to deliver a message," Jessy said.

"Alright, well, what's the message?" Jason asked.

"I'm not supposed to say out here. He said only tell you once inside the house by the fire," Jessy said. Jason thought about it for a minute and realized Marco didn't want the other vampires to hear him. He opened the door wide enough for Jessy to walk in. They walked into the living room together.

"Everyone, this is Jessy," Jason said. "We need to make this a quiet room," Jason whispered to Evelyn. Evelyn lit the candle so that they could talk freely.

"He has confronted Misty and it didn't end well. He said that once she has the baby he is sending her away. He doesn't want to be with her anymore and won't let her stay in the pack either," Jessy said.

Up in Ava's room, she was talking to Mike, trying to make a decision. "I really want to go with him for a while. I want to get to know him. I deserve a chance to get to know my father, right?" Ava asked as she was pacing the floor.

"Yes, you do, but I think it should be done here. Ava, it's not safe out there," Mike said as he stood up and took both her hands.

"But I'm like you and Jason. I'm actually stronger than both of you," Ava said.

"You might be. We honestly don't know yet, Ava. You haven't shown any signs of fangs and won't get your magic for another year," Mike said.

"So I'm just supposed to stay under my brothers and your protection? My dad could protect me too, you know," Ava said. Mike looked at the floor. He knew there was no winning the argument because Ava really wanted to go.

"Alright, fine… but if you go, I am, too. I am going wherever you go," Mike said as he stepped up and hugged her. At that moment, they heard a knock downstairs. They walked into the room as Evelyn lit the candle. She quietly listened to Jessy's message from Marco.

"So my dad is helping us?" Ava said as she walked in behind Jessy.

He turned around to see her standing there. "Ava… Yes, he is. He never wanted to hurt anyone. He just wanted to get to know you," Jessy said.

"Thanks. Tell him to come back over here," Ava said.

"Ava, wait," Jason said.

"No… you wait. He is my father. You know your dad. Now I want to know mine," Ava said as she looked over, and Jessy was staring at her.

"Why are you staring at me?" Ava asked.

"I'm sorry! It's just… well, I have been told how pretty you are, but no one ever said," Jessy said before being cut off.

"Said what?" Mike said as he walked over and put his arm around Ava. "I'm her boyfriend, Mike. Now, why don't you get back to the message," Mike continued.

"Right, sorry. He wants to come back over and talk to everyone about staying in the house to be closer to Ava, but if he can't, he would like to move closer to the home at least," Jessy said as he turned to Jason.

"I can't make that decision. This is my grandmother's home. She gets to decide," Jason said as he looked over at Evelyn.

"I'm assuming you will stay with him since you are his assistant?" Evelyn asked.

"Yes, if that is alright with you?" Jessy asked.

"Tell him to come back over here, and we will discuss it," Evelyn said.

"I will relay your answer," Jessy said as he turned and walked back out the door.

"Are you really considering this?" Sandy asked Evelyn.

"If he is here where we can see him, wouldn't it be better?" Evelyn asked.

"I have to agree. It's hard to set something up with people all around you," Emma said. Ava turned and went back upstairs, followed by Mike.

"My dad is going to stay here. This is my chance to get to know him. This is so perfect," Ava said very excitedly as she walked into her room. Mike walked in behind her and shut the door. "Ava, calm down. We need to talk. You need to be careful. He could be dangerous. I don't want anything to happen to you," Mike suspected.

"What is going to happen? He's my father. He wouldn't hurt me," Ava said as she turned around to face Mike.

"You could be right, but just to be safe, I think you shouldn't be alone with him," Mike said. Ava stepped back away from him.

"You're just like Jason and Henry. Always trying to control me. You can't keep me from my father," Ava said angrily.

"I'm not trying to keep you from him. I just think someone being with you when you're around him is the best idea," Mike said as he stepped toward her.

Ava held her hands up in a stop position, walked around him to the door, and opened it. "Well, I think the best idea is for you to leave my room," Ava said as she pointed out the door.

"Ava," Mike protested.

"I mean it… Get out," Ava said in a raised voice. Jason and Henry heard her and walked up the stairs. As they got to the top of the stairs they saw Mike get pushed out of Ava's room.

"What happened?" Jason asked.

"What did you do to her?" Henry asked in a raised voice as he walked toward Mike.

"Just stop right there, guard dog. I didn't do anything. Is your sister always this stubborn?" Mike asked as he turned to Jason.

"What do you mean?" Jason asked.

"I told her it was a good idea for her not to be alone with her father," Mike said as he turned and looked at Ava's door. Jason kind of laughed a little.

"And how did that go?" Jason asked while smiling. Mike shrugged his shoulders and pointed at the door like well you see what happened. Jason patted him on the shoulder.

"Come in here with us. We don't have any wanted advice for her either. Hey, I have an idea; maybe we should start a club," Jason said sarcastically as he stepped between Mike and Henry, putting his arm around them both to lead them to his room.

The grownups down stairs were still discussing the Marco situation. They were all in their own thought. You could tell they all had an opinion. Some thought it was a good idea, and others hated the thought of him being there. "Well, if we are going to do this can we set some ground rules at least?" Michael asked.

"Like what?" Evelyn asked.

"For starters how about we only let him go in the main rooms, which means the living room, kitchen, and bathroom. I just don't like the idea of him being able to do what he wants. He put my wife in prison, and our kids and I missed so much time with her," Michael said.

"I understand, and I am ok with limiting his wandering to a few rooms. I want to add the basement. Speaking of… Can you guys get the body out of the basement? That's going to be his room," Evelyn said. Branson and Michael looked at each other.

"Yeah, we got it," Branson said as he nudged Michael to follow him as he walked toward the basement. Sky and the others were still in the kitchen waiting to be needed.

"It's crazy that I'm dating a warlock," Sky told Mya.

"What made you think of that?" Mya asked.

"It's just I never thought this would be who I am. I'm helping a witch, warlock, werewolf, and hunter. If my parents only knew?" Sky said as she looked up at Mya. They looked at each other for a minute, and then both busted out laughing.

CHAPTER 12

Everyone was wondering what to do at this point. They had their own opinion of Marco and if he should stay there, but in the end, it would be Evelyn's choice since it was her farm and house. Jason and Henry decided to come back downstairs and Mike followed since Ava was now upset with him. They walked into the living room. The adults were waiting for Marco to show up. Sky heard them coming down and walked in from the kitchen. She waved Jason over to her.

"Everything alright?" Jason asked as he walked up to her.

"Yes, but we should talk," Sky said, walking back into the kitchen with Jason following, looking at all the vampires in the kitchen. Everyone stared back.

"They are all worried about Marco being here, and I have to be honest, Jason, so am I," Sky spoke with concern as she turned and fixed her eyes on him.

"I understand. I don't really like the idea myself. I wish my grandma would have never said for him to come back, but this is better in a way. We will be able to see what he is doing. All of you have great hearing. You could hear what he doesn't want us to hear. I think this is a good plan, but I understand if some of you want to leave." Jason replied with a strong resolve and composure.

"I'm staying with you. I will help in any way I can," Sky comforted him, resting her hand on his.

She then faced the others. "I will not make you stay. This is your choice. I know it is not your fight, but it is Jason's, and that makes it mine, too," she said as she looked at Jason with a look of assurance.

All the vampires exchanged looks, waiting for someone to speak.

Rick jumped off the counter where he had been sitting. "I will stay with you," Rick said. The others nodded in agreement. Sky hugged Jason and led him to the hallway. Once they stepped out of sight, he saw sadness in her eyes.

"What's wrong?" Jason asked.

"I don't want you to get hurt. I love you so much, Jason, and if something happens to you…" Sky said with a shaky voice before being cut off.

"I'm here, I'm fine, don't think like that. We probably won't even have to fight. Marco is coming over here, and he seems nice.

He just wanted to meet Ava. Now that he knows we won't keep her from him, it's going to be fine." Jason wrapped her in his arms.

She looked up at him and kissed him. It felt like a goodbye kiss, but Jason knew she was just worried. She pulled away, but he pulled her back.

"You can't just kiss me like that and run away," Jason chirped and pressed her against him with a huge smile. It relaxed Sky a bit as she laughed and kissed him again. This time, he felt she was a little less stressed and was smiling. Suddenly, there was a knock at the door which made them both jump and look at the door down the hallway. Jason let her go immediately. She went back to the kitchen with the vampires, and he went to the door. He carefully opened the door and saw Marco and Jessy standing there.

"You can come in," Jason invited them in as he stepped aside.

He was trying to be as polite as possible. Marco walked inside and held his hand out to offer him a handshake. Jason obliged, shook his hand, and then walked them to the living room. As they walked in, Evelyn walked over to them.

"Thank you for letting our friends through. As you can see, we were worried at one time things might not end favorable for us." Evelyn spoke first, shaking his hand.

"I can understand that. I do have a big group, and they were not so nice when we first got here. I can assure you it was all without my knowledge. I have talked to my wife and told her she must stop the nonsense because I only wanted to peacefully meet Ava and get to know her." Marco replied.

"Do you think she will listen?" Jason asked as he walked around them and into the living room.

"I will be honest, Jason. I am not sure what she will do. She was not too happy with me. I also told her that once the baby is born, I want her gone. She isn't following me as she should, and she is acting as if she is the leader. From what I have seen, I do believe some of them are following her. This is my fault, and I'm prepared to face the consequences of my actions. I will help you if I can to make this right." Marco said.

Jason just looked at him for a minute, then asked. "Thank you. If you just wanted to meet Ava, why not just call or knock on the door."

"I wanted to make sure she was mine before I did. I also wasn't sure how it would have ended knowing what I did to your mother. I am very sorry for the way I have acted, and the things I have done are unforgivable, so the only thing I can do now is try to make it right if you will let me." Marco answered.

Everyone was quiet. No one knew what to say at this point. If he was telling the truth, he truly sounded sorry, but only time would tell.

"Would you like to sit down?" Evelyn asked.

"Yes, please." Marco walked over to the couch.

He sat down but could tell some of them still didn't trust him.

"Where is my daughter Ava?" he inquired as he sat.

"Oh, I'm sorry. She is in her room. Why don't you run and get her, Jessy?" Evelyn gestured to Jessy and sat beside Marco. "Upstairs, second door on the right," she added as she looked over the back of the couch at him.

Jessy looked at her for a bit, then turned and walked up the stairs. Mike began following him, but Jason held his hand out. Mike turned and went to the kitchen with the other vampires. As Jessy got to her door, he wasn't sure if he should knock or open the door. For a vampire who wasn't used to living a normal life, he was nervous. He decided knocking would be the best idea.

"Ava, it's Jessy… Can I come in?" Jessy talked through the door as he grabbed the doorknob.

"Yes," Ava answered from the other side of the door.

As Jessy opened the door, he immediately smelled blood. He walked in and saw Ava trying to get blood off her hand with a towel.

"Shut the door," Ava ordered.

He shut the door quickly and ran to her. "Ava, what did you do? Are you alright?"

"I'm fine. I was trying to force my vampire side to come out. Figured if I could heal, then it would be safer," she replied, sitting down on the bed.

He could tell there was something wrong. He walked over, sat down beside her, and took her hand. "Ava… Why? You are safe. We will all protect you." He helped her clean her hand.

"My family doesn't want me around you or my dad alone. They don't trust you or him. Someone will be up here any minute to see why we haven't come down." Ava said as she looked up at him.

Jessy was really close. Closer than she thought, and he sensed it too. He got up and stepped back.

"Your hand will be fine. We really should join the others. Your father wants to see you." he quickly shot back.

"Are you scared to be near me or something?" Ava inquired.

"No… I just know my place. You are with someone else, and I'm your father's right hand. I know I can only be your friend."

"Well, if that's how you feel," Ava said as she walked by to the bathroom to clean her hand. She gave him a smile that could drive him crazy, and it did. He quickly turned the other way and bit his lip to keep his words in. There was so much he wanted to say. He has felt a connection with her since he met her. He was trying to ignore the fact he was alone with her.

"OUCH!!" Ava exclaimed from the bathroom.

He ran in to see what was wrong.

"Sorry… I'm fine… the soap just burns." Ava said as she was running her hand under the water.

He walked up behind her, put his arms around her, grabbed her hands, and turned her around. He lifted her hand to his face, which was still bleeding. Just as he kissed her palm, his eyes changed, and she was completely mesmerized by his eyes.

"I don't care if we are allowed," Ava chirped as she leaned in and kissed him. She felt whatever it was between them pull them closer. He picked her up and sat her on the counter, then pulled away from the kiss. He grabbed the bandages and started wrapping her hand for her.

"I can take care of myself, you know?" Ava was smiling.

He just looked at her with a returned smile. After it was done, she wrapped her arms around his neck, and he picked her up off the counter and walked into the bedroom to set her down. Just as he was setting her down, Mike barged in.

"WHAT ARE YOU DOING?! PUT HER DOWN!" he yelled as he bolted towards them.

Jessy threw Ava to the bed to put her out of harm's way. Mike grabbed him and threw him against the wall before he could turn back around to face Mike. Jessy recovered and punched Mike in the face, crashing him to the ground.

"Calm down! I was just trying to help her!" Jessy said. Mike drew back and punched Jessy. "Sure you were helping yourself to her!" Mike retorted as they both stood up.

He charged at Jessy, but Jessy moved, and Mike went crashing into the wall.

Ava jumped up and ran to Jessy. "Are you ok?" she asked, putting her hand on his shoulder.

Jessy put his arm around her and moved her behind him.

"Look, you need to calm down," Jessy turned around and tried to calm Mike, who had turned into a full vampire now. Fangs and eyes changed. "GET OUT OF HERE AVA!" Jessy yelled.

Ava ran to the door, and just as she opened it, Jason stepped in, put up both hands, and used his powers to stop Mike and Jessy from moving.

"What is going on?" Jason inquired, enraged.

"Let me go. I promise I'm calm. But don't let him go." Jessy said.

Jason looked at Ava. He could tell what she wanted by the way she looked at Jessy, so he loosened his grip on him. Jessy fell to the floor. As he stood up, Ava ran to him and helped him up. Jason then let Mike loose too, but used his power to keep him from Jessy.

"Someone start talking now," Jason demanded.

"I walked in on him holding Ava and her legs wrapped around him," Mike almost yelled.

Jason turned to Ava.

"It's not what you think," Ava explained.

"Honestly, it's not," Jessy clarified.

"If it's not what we are thinking, then what is it? Because Ava, you are walking around here in a t-shirt and shorts that are way too short with your legs wrapped around a vampire we know nothing about." Jason ordered.

Ava and Jessy kept quiet, looked at each other, and then towards Mike.

"Fine, I'm letting Mike go," Jason said as he put down his hand. Mike started walking toward them.

"She cut her hand…" Jessy began.

(Mike stopped)

He continued, "I was just helping her clean it up. She couldn't use it to get on and off the counter, so I picked her up."

"Cut her hand how?" Jason interrogated.

"With this," Ava quickly walked over and grabbed a knife from under her mattress.

"Why Ava?" Mike asked.

"I wanted to see if I could heal," Ava replied, walking back over to Jessy.

"And that's all that happened?" Jason inquired, sounding unsure.

Ava looked at Jessy. "Yes," she said, taking a few steps away from Jessy to bring some distance between them.

"Well, let's go back downstairs to see Marco." Jason waved Mike to the front.

"You're just trying to keep an eye on me, right?" Mike asked as he walked by.

"Apparently, I have to," Jason shot back as he followed him.

Jessy stopped Ava for a minute.

"Are you alright?" Jessy asked in a whisper.

"Yes," Ava chirped back as she gave him a quick kiss and then ran in behind Jason.

Jessy stood there smiling for a minute, then followed.

As they walked into the living room, everyone was quiet.

"Should I ask what happened?" Evelyn asked.

"No… It's complicated." Jason replied as he walked over to the couch to sit.

"Hello, Ava. I am glad we will get to spend some time together. Is there anything you want to know about me?" Marco asked as he got up and walked over to her.

"Yes… Why did you take my mom away?" Ava demanded without skipping a beat.

He stood there a minute before answering as if he wasn't sure what to say.

"I was a horrible person back then. I have done many things that I wish now I hadn't. But what I have done before is not who I am now. I would like the chance to prove it to you, Ava. I would never hurt your mother, which is why I just sent her away even then." Marco began.

"That does not excuse the years I spent without her. She missed so much of my life because of what you did." Ava interjected.

"You're right, and for that, I am very sorry. I wish now I would have never done the things I did." Marco said as he turned and looked at Emma. "I am very sorry for what I have done," he added.

"You are forgiven," Emma said.

"The hell he is!" Michael jumped in.

Emma turned to look at him.

"He took you away because you chose me. He needs to pay for what he has done," Michael said as he walked into the center of the room, pointing at Marco.

Emma looked around and then saw the pain in Marco's eyes. "He already has. He has spent this whole time not knowing he had a daughter and missed watching her grow up as well as I," she said.

Marco just looked at her. He knew what she had said was true.

"Well, now, since that is settled, what will we do about your wife? If she is as mean as we think she is, what will we do if she runs with the baby?" Jason asked, trying to ease off the tension.

"I haven't thought about that. I know some of them follow her, but I'm not sure which ones." Marco replied, turning to Jason.

"We could send Jessy in as a spy," Branson suggested.

"What? Why me?" Jessy babbled.

"Well, they know you are close to Marco, so they will believe anything you tell them. You just need to convince his wife that you are on their side instead of his." Branson explained.

"If they think I'm lying, they will kill me," Jessy muttered.

"We can't send him over there," Ava said as she grabbed his hand.

"No offence, Ava, but you have dated three guys in the past week. I think your judgement is a little off." Henry said.

"You fed me to the wolves… Why not Jessy, too? No offence." Mike said as he turned to Henry.

"None taken," Henry smiled.

"Look, we need a real plan so everyone - Think. We need someone on the inside." Jason ordered.

"We need a listening device," Marco suggested.

"Or I could just listen in. I have traveled without my body before, so I'm sure I can do it again," Jason said as he walked over to Evelyn.

He sat down on the couch and got ready.

"What if it doesn't work?" Henry asked inquisitively.

"It's worth a try," Jason reassured as he leaned back on the couch.

He got lost in thought. Thinking about everything that had happened. He was a warlock, Henry a werewolf, Sky a vampire, and Ava a witch/vampire. How did his life get this crazy, and just how strong would his powers get? He felt a shiver down his body, and he opened his eyes. He was in Marco's old tent. Something felt off, though. It felt too real. He walked over to the table and was able to pick up a piece of paper sitting on top. Suddenly, he realized he wasn't there in his mind. He was really there. He started to travel back but then figured maybe he could creep around and eavesdrop. They needed to know what was going on. He slipped from the tent and went into the bushes. He crouched down and crawled down the bush line to the center of the camp. There, he saw a large group of vampires gathered around the fire, acting like animals. They were aggressive even with each other, completely undisciplined – feral. He then saw Misty walk out of a tent and walk up to the group.

"What are you doing? How will we kill him if you guys are just going to kill each other? I need him gone if I'm going to lead and pick one of you to lead with me. I want his daughter dead as well, so save your strength because it's going to be one hell of a fight." Misty addressed as she turned around toward the tent. They all walked over to her and started kissing her hands and arms as she walked back to the tent. She then pulled away and walked back inside. At this point, he knew one thing. She was going to kill Marco and take over. He needed to warn them, but he also needed to see what else was going on. He could hear others talking inside a different tent. He walked over to get closer to hear them.

"We need to do something. She is going to take over, and we will all have to kneel to her or be slaughtered. She wants to be like a queen."

"She thinks she is one."

"We could just leave."

"And go where… Do you know someone we don't know about? Get real."

"We have been in the pack for so long we don't even know anyone outside the pack."

Jason had heard enough. The vampires in this tent didn't like her as much as they didn't. He slowly walked around the side of the tent and popped inside. They all jumped up with fangs out and lunged at him.

"Stop! We want her gone as well, and we sure don't want her to lead. Maybe we can help each other?" Jason asked.

They all looked at each other and backed up a little. "What do you have in mind?" They asked. Jason turned around and closed the tent.

"We have been trying to figure out how to listen in on her plans. Marco wants to take the baby and make her leave." Jason said.

"That might be a little hard." One of the vampires said.

"What do you mean?" Jason inquired.

"She is planning to leave with the baby and have the pack attack the house. It's supposed to happen just before morning. We are under specific orders to kill Ava and Marco and anyone else that gets in the way," the vampire informed.

"Can you be my eyes and ears and let me know when she starts gathering everyone up?" Jason asked.

"Sure, but we were all thinking about leaving," the vampire replied.

"I overheard the talk you guys were having. If you help me, you can stay here in the barn. You won't have to stay with them anymore. You can live a good life as long as you stop killing." Jason tried assuring him.

The vampires looked at each other. "Five vampires living in a barn… what could go wrong?" One of them said with a small laugh.

Jason laughed as well and pulled his phone out of his pocket. "Do any of you have a phone?" he asked.

One of them took a phone out and handed it to him. He entered his number and texted himself. "Text me updates as much as you can," he said as he handed the phone back. He then traveled home to tell the others.

He appeared in the living room, and everyone ran to him.

"You were only supposed to Astro project, not go in person," Ava said as she ran up and hugged him.

"Are you alright?" Evelyn asked.

"Where is Marco?" Jason asked.

Evelyn pointed behind him. Jason turned around and Marco was standing right behind him.

"I am guessing you saw my wife?" Marco asked.

"I saw her, and just to let you know, I think she is cheating on you. But what's even more important, she plans to run with the baby." Jason informed.

"I will kill her!" Marco retorted as he marched to the door.

"Stop!" Jason said.

Marco turned around reluctantly.

"I have some people on the inside now. I offered them a place to stay in the barn for their help because they want out of your pack." Jason spoke carefully.

"So they are on our side?" Mike dubiously asked.

"Not all of them, but at least five are," Jason said as he walked over to sit down on the couch.

"She plans to leave and have them all attack us in the morning," he added.

"So what do we plan to do?" Mike asked.

"We could kill her," Sky pitched in.

"She is pregnant… We can't just kill her." Henry said.

"What if she went into labor before she left? She would have to stay through labor. Then we could take the baby." Evelyn said as she looked at Emma.

"Well, that's a thought, but how do we get her to go into labor?" Emma asked.

"Is there a spell for that too?" Jason asked.

"Well, probably, but I'm thinking spicy food," Evelyn said.

"That's what did it for me," Emma said.

"We feed her," Evelyn said as she walked to the kitchen.

Jason followed her. "Feed her what?"

"I'm thinking spicy barbeque chicken," Evelyn suggested.

"Spice works almost every time," Emma added as she followed them, too.

"Marco should be asked before we just do this," Jason said.

"Well… go ask him," Evelyn prompted as she walked over to the fridge.

Jason turned and walked back to the living room. Jason walked over to Marco.

"I know you heard my mom and grandma talking. They want to feed her spicy food to see if it will make her go into labor. I can get it to her. I can hand it to one of the people on the inside, and they can give it to her." Jason explained.

"I want her dead. As soon as the baby is born, I will kill her —
do it." Marco said as he looked at Jason.

He then walked over to the couch and sat down. Jason walked
back into the kitchen. Evelyn already had the chicken on the table
and was fixing it up to go in the oven. They both looked up at Jason.

"He said to do it," Jason said as he walked over to them. "I could
have taken care of that," he added as he sat his hands on the table.

"No… save your strength. We will need it later," Evelyn pitched
in as she turned to put the pan in the oven.

Back in the living room, everyone is on edge. They all knew
what would happen soon, yet no one wanted to talk about it. Henry,
on the other hand, was slowly losing his mind. He felt like this was
all just as crazy as a dream.

"Are we out of our minds?" Henry said as he ran his hands
across his face and brushed his hair back with frustration.

Everyone turned to look at him. Henry looked around the room
at everyone.

"Doesn't anyone else think this is just crazy? Just the other day
I was a normal teenager that couldn't wait to get out of this town.
Now I find out I'm a werewolf and my best friend is a warlock, and
his sister is a witch and vampire, and now we are trying to make a
lady go into labor so we can kill her. Oh, and let's not forget that it's
my best friend's sister's dad's wife. I mean, seriously, is all this not
crazy to anyone? When will this nightmare end?" Henry quipped
and exclaimed as he paced around the living room, walked over, put

his back against the wall, and slid down till he was sitting on the floor.

He then put his head in his hands and sat quietly. Sandy walked over to him. She bent down and grabbed his hand. He looked up at her.

"We have to do this," Sandy tried to convince him.

"I know, Mom, but it doesn't make it any easier. If we don't kill her, she will kill us. I get it. I just don't like it. I miss my old life. Jason made a good point. Our old lives are over." Henry said as he looked down at the floor.

"Yes, you're right, but your new life could be so much better. We just have to get through this, and then it will get better." Sandy assured.

Henry looked at her in disbelief. Jason then walked back into the living room. He looked down at Henry.

"What happened to you?" Jason asked.

"I had a mental breakdown, but I'm good," Henry said as he stood up.

"Good because the food is almost done. Now we have to figure out how to get her to eat it and go into labor." Jason quickly informed.

Emma and Evelyn walked into the room with the food. "That won't be hard. Pregnant women are always hungry." Evelyn informed.

"Hand it to me. I will go back and give this to the ones on our side, and then they can give it to her." Jason held out his arms. He then pulled his phone out to text them.

"Meet me in your tent. I have something for you." Jason texted. He then traveled to the tent. As he appeared, the tent was empty. He sat the food down as soon as the vamp came in.

"What is that?" The vamp asked.

"Just spicy chicken. My grandma said it can sometimes make a pregnant woman go into labor. We need you to give it to her." Jason said.

"So we are wanting her to have the baby?" The vamp asked.

"Yes, because once she has the baby, Marco is going to take care of her," Jason said.

"Good plan… Yours?" The vamp asked.

"No, but it's the only plan we have. What's your name, by the way?" Jason asked.

"Johnny," he said.

"I'm going to head back. Text me if it works." Jason said.

"Will do," Johnny confirmed.

Jason stepped back and disappeared. Johnny took the chicken to Misty.

"I have something for you. We made it over the fire." Johnny said as he sat it down on the small table.

"That's very sweet of you…But you take a piece first." Misty walked over, picked up a piece, and handed it to Johnny.

Johnny took a bite. "That tastes so good. You are going to love it."

Misty sat down and started eating it. Johnny pulled his phone out and texted Jason. "She is eating it. I hope this works."

He then walked over to the others. They all went into the tent so that Johnny could fill them in on the plan. Their number had grown from 5 to 11, and more were still joining them. There were so many against Misty, and they did not want her to lead.

"Jason is also going to let us all stay in the barn after this is over. We won't have to be on the run anymore and no more tents." Johnny happily exclaimed. "I'm trusting you all to keep this quiet and only recruit those you really trust," he added with a smile.

CHAPTER 13

Jason got back to the house, and everyone was waiting for him. "I gave it to him. How long does it take it to work?" Jason asked.

"It depends. Sometimes it doesn't work at all, but other times it does," Evelyn answered.

Just about that time, Jason got the text from Johnny. "I am hoping the same, but if it does, let us know as soon as possible. Someone must be there to ensure the baby stays with Marco." Jason wrote in the text. Jason put his phone away and looked up at the others. "Johnny just texted me and said she took it. If this doesn't work, do we have another plan?" Jason asked.

"If it doesn't work, we just have to find a way to keep her here so that she goes into labor while still here," Emma said.

"That might be hard to do. She is very good at taking over, and with the vamps willing to follow her, she can and will leave," Tim added.

"Maybe we should just kidnap her," Branson suggested.

"How would we do that? We can't bring her here. She would be too close to Ava and kill Ava the first chance she got," Jason said.

"What if we put her in the barn?" Branson asked.

"She wouldn't be in the same house as Ava, but she also wouldn't be there to take over the other vamps, so it might be a good plan B," Sandy said.

"Okay, if she doesn't go into labor, we kidnap her. This has to happen before morning, or they are all coming here, and there are more of them than us," Michael said.

"There are a lot of Ifs going around. Not sure I like the odds," Henry said in a concerned voice.

Jason looked at him and then looked back at everyone else. "I guess we should hope she goes into labor then," Jason said.

"We also need to talk about you staying here with Ava," Evelyn said as she looked at Marco.

"We do. I don't want to cause any trouble. I just don't want to miss any more time with my daughter. I am not trying to take your place. I know you have raised her and will always be her dad, but I'm her father, too, and I just want to know her," Marco said as he looked at Michael. "Once this is over, you can stay in the barn with your pack until we find another way for us all to be here," Evelyn proposed.

At that moment, Sky walked in, followed by Mya. "I have a stipulation to all this. I am a leader in this area, and we have rules that must be followed. We will not allow another pack to move into the area unless they follow our ways. We do not bite people. It is unacceptable. We own a blood drive, which will be more than enough to feed us all. We usually have way more than needed and donate to the hospitals. We will supply you with blood in exchange for work. I am not going to take over your pack. Instead, I'm requesting we become allies. We cannot allow you to stay in this area if you do not agree to these terms," Sky mentioned her terms. Marco looked at Tim and Jessy.

"I would also like to add that if any of your pack kills a mortal we will kill them," Mya said as she stepped up next to Sky. Marco looked back at them.

"I accept and will talk it over with my pack. Anyone that does not agree will be banished to live alone," Marco agreed.

Everyone sat for a while, wondering what was going on with Misty. "Where is Ava? Has anyone seen or talked to her in a while?" Jason asked.

"I'm sure she is in the kitchen," Sandy answered.

Sky came running into the living room and pantingly said, "No, she isn't. I don't know where she is."

Jessy stood by the stairs and ran up to Ava's room. As Jessy threw open the door, Ava was lying in bed asleep, and he saw someone outside the window. The concoction woke her up. She saw them too and screamed.

"SOMEONE WAS OUTSIDE HER WINDOW AND JUST JUMPED DOWN!" Jessy screamed, too, to grab attention. Everyone ran outside while Jessy stayed with Ava. He pulled a chair over to the window and sat down.

"Who was that?" Ava asked.

"I don't know, but you can go back to sleep. I won't leave this spot," Jessy comforted her. Ava laid back down and turned over, away from the window. She was scared to look out for it. She didn't know if she could go back to sleep, but she knew she would be okay since Jessy was there. Everyone returned inside.

"I can't believe they got away," Henry said.

"It's ok they didn't get Ava. I'm going to go check on her," Jason said. As he got to her room, he saw Jessy. Ava finally fell back asleep, and Jason waved to Jessy and signaled to come to the door. Jessy shook his head no and pointed to the window. Jason knew Jessy was refusing to leave that spot to ensure she was safe. Jason gave a gentle wave and went back downstairs.

"Jessy is staying with her. He has a chair by the window to watch for anyone," Jason informed.

"You need to text Johnny and find out what he can find out," Tim said.

Jason pulled his phone out and texted him, "Do you know who came over here? They were at Ava's window and got away."

He put his phone away while they waited for an answer.

"May I go up to sit with Ava?" Marco asked as he looked at Evelyn.

"I think that should be alright," Evelyn agreed.

Marco went up the stairs to Ava's room. At that moment, Jason's phone beeped. Jason read the text aloud: "She planned to take Ava with her as she leaves. She has now decided the best way to get back at Marco is to turn Ava against him."

"She will not be taking Ava anywhere," Tim said.

Marco walked into Ava's room and walked over to Jessy. "Could you tell who it was?" Marco asked.

"Sadly, no, and if I could have got to the window in time, I would have killed them," Jessy answered.

"You heard what they said, right?" Marco asked another question.

"Yes… they want Ava. She is going to take her away from here to hurt you," Jessy replied.

"She wants to take me away?" Ava asked as she sat up in bed.

"We didn't mean to wake you," Marco apologetically said.

"I was already awake. Why would she think I would go with them?" Ava asked.

"I don't think she will give you a choice. If she thinks it will hurt me, she will just kidnap you and keep you away from me," Marco explained.

"She could do that by killing me," Ava said.

"It wouldn't be the same. To know you are alive somewhere and not be able to find you and wondering what she was doing to you would be far worse torture than her killing you and me knowing you're at peace," Marco said.

"Jessy, can you give us a moment?" Marco asked Jessy.

Jessy nodded, got up, and walked out the door. Marco sat in the chair, and Ava moved to the end of the bed. "Your grandma has agreed to let me stay in the barn, and I want to know if you're ok with that?" Marco asked.

"So you can get to know me?" Ava asked.

"Yes… I want to get to know you and build a bond. I don't kill anymore, but you should know that everything people have said about me is true. I realized I needed to change as soon as I found out about you. I couldn't stay angry at the world," Marco said.

"I would really like to get to know you as well," Ava added.

"Good, then I will stay," Marco said.

"Will Jessy and Tim stay, too?" Ava asked.

"Yes… they are with me everywhere I go," Marco answered.

Ava just sat there looking at the floor. Marco could tell she had a lot on her mind. "What's wrong?" Marco asked.

"All of this is my fault. They are only here because of you, and you are only here because of me. If I weren't here, then no one would be here hurting my family. My life has put everyone in this house in danger, and I can't help but feel like my life isn't worth all this," Ava sobbed.

"You can't think like that, Ava," Jason said as he entered the room. Ava looked up and saw him standing inside the door.

"Why? You put your life on the line all the time. Why can't I say how I feel? Is it better for me to hold it all in Jason? I'm 15 and a vampire witch. I should be hanging out with my friends and worrying about normal teenage things, but instead, I worry about if the next time my brother leaves, will he come back, or if the next vamp that comes over here will kill me and my family for trying to protect me. I haven't talked to my friends in days and won't because I have no idea what to tell them when they ask where I have been," Ava said as she stood up and walked over to Jason.

"Ava," Jason said before being cut off.

"Don't Ava me. You know I'm right. All of you do. I'm just the only one willing to say it," Ava said as she walked into the bathroom. Jason stood there quietly, not knowing what to say.

"I will have Jessy sit in the room. Maybe it is best for us to let her be," Marco said as he got up and walked by Jason out the door.

Jason stood there for a minute and then followed him. Ava sat in the bathroom crying for a long time.

Marco met Jessy downstairs and had him go sit in Ava's room again. At that moment, there was a text from Johnny. Jason grabbed his phone. "It worked. Misty's water broke. She will have the baby soon. Johnny says she has told the others that they will not attack until the baby is born. This means she will be running with the baby soon," Jason announced.

"Labor can take minutes to hours and sometimes days," Evelyn informed.

"Mom is right. The question is, who is going to go over and take it," Emma asked.

"I will," Marco said as he sat down on the couch.

"I will have Johnny text me when the baby is born. We will have to move quickly. Tim, go upstairs and help Jessy because they will be coming for Ava when the baby is born," Jason ordered. Tim ran up the stairs to tell them the news.

As he walked in, Ava was still in the bathroom. "I heard. Let's board this window back up so it will make it harder on them," Jessy said. They put all of it on the window and sat on Ava's bed. As Ava sat in the bathroom crying, she wondered why this was her life. Why did it get so complicated? She just wanted to be normal and have a normal life, but she knew she couldn't do that here. She looked up at the bathroom window and decided she would do what she had to do. She slowly walked to the window, opened it, and climbed out onto the roof. She looked for a way down and found a tree limb hanging over the roof, so she climbed into the tree and down and ran off into the woods.

Everyone was waiting patiently for sunrise, which was about an hour away. It had been hours since they heard from Johnny. "What will we do if they get in the house?" Emma asked.

"First thing, I'm taking Mike and Ava to his house, and they will wait it out there. We have to get Ava out of harm's way," Jason said as he looked at Mike.

"I will take care of her even though she isn't going to like it," Mike said.

"Kill all of them. If they are willing to hurt people, they shouldn't be allowed to live," Marco ordered.

"I think you should try to win them over first if possible. The more that are on our side, the better," Jason suggested.

"What if they are not willing to talk? We can't just make them listen," Henry argued.

"In that case, we will go with Marco's plan. Just kill them. Maybe if enough of them die, the others will stop and listen," Jason said.

"I would like to go with Mike and Ava to help just in case they find them. One of us can fight while the other runs with Ava," Mya said.

"That's a good plan," Jason agreed. Jason heard his phone beep and looked at the text, and it was Johnny. It says: "Call me." Jason announced as he looked around the room, confused. He sat the phone down on the table in the living room, called Johnny, and put it on speaker.

"Jason? Can you hear me?" Johnny asked. They could hear a lot of background noise.

"Yes, but what is all that?" Jason asked.

"Chaos… complete chaos. There is fighting and everyone is killing each other. I'm trying to stop them, but there is just too much. I don't know what to do," Johnny said. Panic in his voice was evident.

"Why are they all fighting?" Jason asked.

"Because we are without a leader. She is gone. We don't know when or how, but Misty and about 27 vampires are gone. Everyone is losing it, fighting for leadership. We will not make it if this doesn't stop," Johnny answered.

"WHERE IS THE BABY!" Marco yelled.

"We can't find it either. I don't even know if she had it. I know there is a lot of blood in her tent. Something happened. I'm guessing she had it, but I can't be sure," Johnny said.

"I'm coming. I will stop this," Marco said.

"Good because I can't stop them. I have tried. Oh, and Jason, is Ava still there?" Johnny asked. Marco stopped before walking out the door.

"Yes… I think she is still in the bathroom. She is very upset with us. Why do you ask?" Jason asked.

"Because we can all smell her. Her scent is everywhere out here," Johnny said before the call was cut. Jason looked at the stairs.

"CHECK FOR AVA!" Jason yelled as he ran toward the stairs. Jessy and Tim heard him. Tim tried to open the bathroom, but it was locked.

"MOVE!" Jessy yelled as he kicked open the door. They ran inside to find the bathroom window open and a note on the mirror.

"No one else is dying for me. Don't look for me," Ava wrote. Jason came running in. Jessy pointed at the mirror. Jason ran back downstairs with Tim and Jessy right behind him.

"Ava ran away," Jason shouted.

"Oh my God. Misty is out there. If she catches Ava," Emma said as she started crying.

"She won't. We will find her," Jason said calmly, trying to comfort his mom.

"I will track her," Branson offered his help.

"Anyone willing to help, come with us," Jason said.

"I will calm down the pack so no one goes hunting for her. Tim and Jessy come with me. I might need help to stop them," Marco said as he walked out the door. Jason's group took off behind him and ran into the woods. Jason, Henry, and Mike were in one group.

"We can have two groups. I can smell her, so I can lead one group. Branson can lead the other group," Henry said.

They all split off to look. Branson had Sky and Mya in his group. Evelyn and Michael were at the house using magic to try and find her while Emma sat crying on the couch. The vamps from Sky's pack stayed in the house to protect them while Sandy and her wolf pack guarded the outside of the house.

The sun was beginning to rise, and it was getting brighter and easier for everyone to see. Both groups were closing in on Ava. "The scent is really strong this way," Henry said. They walked deep into the woods to the river, where Henry lost the scent. "I can't smell her here," Henry informed.

"That's because she went into the river," Branson said from behind them.

"I followed a trail all the way here. She got into the river. You can't follow her with a scent through the water." Branson continued.

"Can you find her trail again on the other side?" Jason asked.

"I can try," Branson said.

"If you get me a trail, I can follow the scent," Henry said. They all jumped in the river and started looking for any signs of Ava. They walked in both directions, and Branson looked very hard. Henry kept catching a scent and losing it. "Why do I smell her for a couple of feet and then back to the water?" Henry asked.

"Because Ava is very smart. She is slowing us down by making us think she crossed the river, which then leads us back to the river. She will be long gone by the time we find the right trail," Branson answered.

"So what do we do?" Jason asked.

"Travel to her. Just think about Ava and go. Bring her back," Henry proposed to Jason. Jason closed his eyes and thought of Ava but suddenly opened his eyes.

"What's wrong?" Henry asked.

"I don't know. I can't find her. It's like she blocked herself from me somehow," Jason answered.

"She doesn't have any magic. How would she do that?" Mya asked.

"There is a spell you can use to enchant an object to shield you from magic. Sandy told me about it and showed me the necklace. But Ava can't do it. Someone would have had to make it for her," Jason answered.

Sky walked over to him and asked, "Jason, is that necklace you gave me enchanted?"

"Yes… that's why I made it for you. Sky, where is your necklace?" Jason asked as he turned and looked at her.

"I didn't know. Ava was scared, and I put the necklace on her to cheer her up and asked her to keep it safe for me," Sky said with regret and conviction.

Jason could see she felt very bad. "It's my fault, not yours. I should have told you what it was," Jason said as he walked up and hugged her.

"Your grandma isn't going to find her with magic either. We need to let them know," Branson said as he turned towards the house. They all slowly walked back towards the house. Sky was crying as she felt so bad. Ava was like her little sister, and she loved her.

When they walked into the house, Emma was still crying. "Did you find her?" Emma asked as she stood up and ran to Jason. He grabbed his Mom, hugged her, and started to cry himself. "No, Mom, we didn't," Jason said.

Sky started to cry even more. "It's all my fault," Sky said in between her sobs.

"How is it your fault?" Evelyn asked as he walked over to Sky.

"I gave it to her. I didn't know," Sky said.

"Didn't know what?" Emma asked as she walked over to Sky.

"It's not her fault, it's mine… Sandy told me about her necklace, so I made one for Sky. I didn't tell her what it was because that was before she knew about me. She gave it to Ava to make her feel better," Jason explained.

"Meaning, Magic won't work on her now," Michael said as he slammed the book shut. He walked over to Jason. "WHAT WERE YOU THINKING? THIS WAS HARD ENOUGH WITHOUT ADDING MORE ISSUES!" Michael yelled.

"Don't yell at him. He was trying to protect Sky. The same way you would have protected me," Emma said.

"We won't be able to find her. She went through the water and covered her tracks well," Branson said.

"We just need more people. More groups," Henry said.

"Everyone, just calm down; it might take a while, but we will find her," Sandy said. She ran outside to her pack, and they went out to search.

"We should call Marco and let him know," Evelyn said. Jason pulled his phone out and called Johnny.

"We need to talk to Marco," Jason said.

"Let me find him," Johnny said.

"Hello, this is Marco," Marco said.

"This is Jason… We can't find Ava. We have looked everywhere, and Sandy and her pack are out there now," Jason said.

Marco was very quiet for a minute. "I will send a few people I trust to look for her," Marco said before hanging up.

"Marco is sending a few people out, too," Jason announced as he looked at everyone. "See, we will find her," Evelyn said.

"Before Misty?" Sky asked. No one said anything but they were all thinking it. If Misty finds her first, they know she will be killed or taken.

"We have all been up all night. Let's get some rest. We can't help her if we are exhausted," Evelyn said.

Marco was working on gathering up people from his pack. "We need to look for Ava. I need people I can trust to bring her back safely," Marco said.

"I have a few people that were willing to follow Jason, so I'm sure they will help," Johnny said.

"Gather them and bring them to me," Marco ordered.

Johnny ran off to get them all together and brought them to Marco. "These are the ones I trust the most," Johnny said.

"I need you all to go out and help find my daughter. Bring her back to me. If you see Misty, take the baby and kill her. I want my family back. Jessy and Tim are going with you," Marco said. No one questioned him, and he set out to find Ava. The trail led them back to the river, where they all split into two-man teams. After searching for hours, they started to smell blood. They followed the scent and found Ava. She had slipped and landed on a rock and cut her hand. She tried to run, but Tim grabbed her.

"Don't run, Ava. Misty has left and is in these woods somewhere as well. Let us save you before she kills you," Tim requested.

"We have to take her to Marco," Jessy said. They all set out and headed back to camp.

Sandy's group was also on her trail, but on the way, they found Misty. She had many vamps with her, and they moved slowly. Sandy then saw the baby. It had been born, and Misty looked weak. "We could take her," one of the wolves said.

"No… Misty might be weak, but they are not," Sandy stopped them. They watched the group move through the trees and out of sight. "Let's head back and tell them we found her," Sandy said.

Sandy's pack got back to the house, and everyone was asleep. She sent a wolf to tell Marco about Misty. Then Sandy woke up Evelyn. "We did not find Ava, but we did find Misty. I sent a wolf to tell Marco," Sandy said.

Jason had woken up and heard her. "Was the baby with her?" Jason asked as he walked into the room.

"Yes… and about 20 other vamps. We couldn't get the baby," Sandy said.

"Marco will go after her. I hope Ava doesn't get caught in the crossfire," Jason said.

Just then, Sandy's wolf came running in. "They found Ava. She showed up with the pack as I told Marco about Misty," The wolf said.

"We have to go get her. I will wake up everyone," Jason said. He started waking up the others, and the front door flew open. Jason turned around, and it was Tim.

"They are leaving. They are going after Misty," Tim informed.

"I knew they would," Jason said.

"You don't understand. They are all going." Tim said.

"What are you saying?" Jason asked.

"Marco asked Ava if she wanted to go with him. She said yes." Tim said. Jason looked very upset and disappeared. He went to the camp and looked around. They were all gone. Even the ones that wanted to stay. They had left and taken Ava. Jason went back to the house. "They are gone. I can try to travel to her, but I'm sure Marco will be able to block me." Jason informed.

"So what do we do now?" Emma asked.

"We do everything we can to find her and bring her home," Michael said. Jason and Henry walked outside, and Tim followed.

"Why did you come here instead of leaving with them?" Jason asked.

"I told you I don't like Marco; he has done terrible things. I was hoping we could save Ava before he left, but I guess he counted on you showing up when the wolf saw Ava, so they ran," Tim said.

"I guess we should go look for her together," Jason said.

"We are the weirdest friends ever. Warlock, werewolf, and a vampire. What could go wrong?" Henry said with a sarcastic voice. They all laughed a little.

"I know she is safe with him, but we need to get her back," Jason said.

"Road trip?" Henry asked.

Jason looked at Henry and then looked at Tim. They all stood up and went inside. "We are leaving and not coming back without Ava," Jason said. Evelyn grabbed Jason and hugged him. She started to cry, and Sandy did the same to Henry. Emma walked over and hugged Jason as well.

"Bring my daughter home," Emma said as she let go. Sky walked up and kissed Jason goodbye.

"Keep my family safe for me. I will stay in touch and see you all soon," Jason said. They all watched as the boys got in the truck and drove out of sight. They knew it would be a while before they saw the boys again.